"Men! You need my help and you're going to get it."

With that, Lilly grabbed Cort's arm and towed him toward the back door.

"You make men sound like a dirty word," he said, giving no resistance to her as she opened the back door and led the way into the warm house. He knew he might regret this.

"Well, you have to understand my upbringing. My grandmas hadn't exactly met the best of the species."

Cort helped Lilly remove her coat. In her jeans and turtleneck sweater, she was a charming picture with her girl-next-door beauty.

The girl next door to him.

Books by Debra Clopton

Love Inspired

The Trouble with Lacy Brown #318
And Baby Makes Five #346

*Mule Hollow

DEBRA CLOPTON

was a 2004 Golden Heart finalist in the inspirational category. *And Baby Makes Five* is her second novel with Love Inspired. She makes her home in Texas with her family.

AND BABY
MAKES FIVE

DEBRA CLOPTON

Steeple
Hill®

Published by Steeple Hill Books™

STEEPLE HILL BOOKS

**Steeple
Hill**®

ISBN 0-373-87364-6

AND BABY MAKES FIVE

Copyright © 2006 by Debra Clopton

Printed in U.S.A.

Teach me to do Your will, for You are my God;
may Your good Spirit lead me on level ground.
—*Psalms* 143:10

This book is dedicated to my sons:
Chase and Kris.
I love you.
May you always have as much joy in your lives
as you've brought to mine.
Dream big, guys.
You can do all things through Christ who
strengthens you.

Chapter One

Samantha, bless her weird, little, mischievous soul, was up to no good.

Lilly Tipps knew this. She knew it all the way down to the tips of her water-retaining, swollen big toes. Trouble was brewing, and Samantha was the cause of it.

Again!

Scanning the icy darkness, Lilly scrunched her brow and absently massaged her tight stomach as another Braxton-Hicks contraction started building in its intensity. The false labor pains had been hitting her off and on for the past two weeks, but tonight…oohhh! Lilly took a deep breath, then exhaled slowly. Tonight they were stronger than usual and it was all because of Samantha.

In an effort to ignore the pain, Lilly pulled her coat closed over her rotund tummy, flipped her collar up about her ears, then settled her red wool cap over her corkscrew curls. She concentrated on the task at hand as the pain, more of a nuisance than anything, peaked.

"I must admit, sweet baby…" she said aloud—she'd taken up chatting or singing to her baby early in the pregnancy. She knew it was a good thing to let her child learn her voice, and also, it was nice to have someone to talk to other than Samantha. "I'd trade my whole cache of banana Laffy Taffy and half my chocolate-covered peanut stash for a man to help search for Samantha." She inhaled deeply and let it out slowly. "I'm so not wanting to wander around in this freezing weather looking for an ornery old donkey."

It was a little odd. Not everyone had a donkey cohabiting with them, and Lilly was finding that keeping the old girl home was a major job, especially for a single gal eight months pregnant and growing by the second.

Buck up, Lilly. You volunteered to take her on.

"Yes, I did," she said into the wind as stinging prickles of ice misted across her bare face. It was obvious that Samantha had decided to take her aging little body up the road to her old homestead. It was also obvious that the only one to fetch her back was Lilly. Pregnant or not. False contractions or not.

So be it. Surrendering to her decision, Lilly waddled from the protection of the barn into the icy wind toward her truck. She sympathized with Samantha, she really did. Being forced to give up your home and move would be hard, even if it was only down the road. Lilly had been born and raised in Mule Hollow and couldn't imagine living anywhere else. Samantha needed to learn Lilly's home was now her home. Containing the donkey was an almost impossible task, since she was like the great Houdini, escaping constantly.

Lilly bit her lip in concentration. She had to find a way to keep her little friend home. It was for Samantha's own good. If half of what Lilly had heard circulating in Mule Hollow about the new owner of Samantha's homestead were true, then trespassing on her former stomping grounds could very possibly get Samantha shot.

Lilly at last reached her truck without mishap. The pangs had disappeared for the moment, thank goodness. Why couldn't these fake labor pains hit during the day while she was in her warm house designing her cattle sales catalogs? At least then she could stop and relax until they passed. But the pains had to start in the middle of the night, just like Samantha misbehaving. Lilly sighed, glad the contractions had given her a reprieve. She wrestled open the door of her ancient truck, then hoisted herself into the high seat, which was no easy feat with her small, roly-poly stature. Once up there, she had to rest for a second before she could proceed. After a few moments she caught her breath, twisted the key and, to her dismay, listened as the engine rumbled to life.

"Why, thank You, Lord, for Your steadfastness," she muttered. "I guess this is a sign that I truly do have to go on down there and get myself shot." Looking heavenward, she smiled. God knew her. They'd been building a solid relationship for the past few months and she realized she wasn't hiding anything from Him. He already understood the truck's reliability hadn't been priority this evening.

She was more afraid that if Cort Wells caught Samantha, he might tan not only her wrinkled hide, but Lilly's, too.

However, she wasn't about to let rumors color her views of the man. A person couldn't escape the gossip in Mule Hollow—where some towns had a grapevine, Mule Hollow had an entire vineyard. Mr. Wells was being discussed in the feed store and at the gas pump, especially the gas pump. Just yesterday, minding her own business pumping unleaded into her truck, Applegate Thornton and Stanley Orr stood not three feet from her, openly debating what would cause a man to have such a scowl etched between his eyebrows. That scowl was legendary, and though she'd never witnessed it, evidently it hadn't wavered during any of his dealings with the locals in the short time since he'd moved to town.

Why, even the ladies at Heavenly Inspirations Hair Salon had mentioned it. If they noticed it then it must be something, because Lacy Brown, the owner, didn't like gossip at all and certainly didn't put up with it. Apparently she had said to the group that they all needed to pray about what kind of problem would make a man want to walk around glaring at people like that.

Lilly started praying. She prayed that Samantha would behave and they could sneak away without meeting the man. Of course, that wasn't very Christian. It was more of an all-out rebellion against her duty as one of His. She sighed. Hermit or no hermit, she still had to be neighborly. It seemed she was always failing at that particular portion of her renewed walk with the Lord.

Then again, the grannies had taught her well the many reasons to excuse bad behavior when it came to interacting with men. Two generations of grannies, plus her mother, who'd all had their hearts trampled by the men they'd loved, had no sympathy where a man's feelings were concerned.

Great-Granny Shu-Shu literally hated men. Granny Gab would have strung a man up by his toes and never shown him any type of common courtesy. There was a time when the men of Mule Hollow practically walked across the street when her grannies went in for supplies.

Over the years, because of the intervention of sweet-hearted Granny Bunches, who was really her great-aunt, they'd come to tolerate each other in order to live in the same small community. But still, all her life Lilly had been taught to believe the worst about men.

Old habits that ingrained were hard to break.

But since her change of heart, her upbringing was no excuse to show bad behavior to her new neighbor.

Having let the engine warm sufficiently, Lilly rammed the heater lever to the on position, but made no move to engage the gears.

Of course… She paused, an idea blooming in her mind. It was late and Cort Wells would be sleeping like a normal person, unlike herself. She'd simply creep in, grab Samantha and scoot right back home.

The man need never know they'd been around.

Surely he was snoring in a warm bed, totally ignorant of the world around him.

Okay. Okay, Lord. Sucking in a breath, Lilly squared her shoulders. No one could be all that bad. The man was a horse trainer, for goodness' sake, not an ax murderer. Why, as she kept saying, she should already have popped over there and introduced herself. He was after all her closest neighbor within ten miles.

If she'd been able to afford Leroy's place, then Cort Wells wouldn't have been her neighbor. She'd have been all the way out there, forgotten and bliss-fully alone, just the way she liked it. But you weren't able to afford the ranch, she thought, and now you have a new neighbor, and so be it, tonight or in the next few days, you are going to have to make his ac-quaintance one way or another. God would have her stretch past her own desire and reach for His purpose.

That's what she'd been learning—that's what she was striving to do.

With that said, and before she chickened out, Lilly stomped hard on the gas pedal, grimacing when the truck lurched forward.

Again Lilly frowned, thinking about the ax-murderer portion of her imaginings about her ill-tempered, large, glowering grinch of a neighbor.

She was heading to his house in the dark of night. Truth was Cort Wells wasn't an ax murderer—thus far. But he hadn't met hairy old meddling Samantha.

Yet.

Cort Wells figured his frozen ears were about as hard as a block of ice and ten times colder than ears had any right to be. His fingers were numb. His nose was colder than his dog's after a dip in the fishpond behind the barn. After three hours of hiding inside the horse stables, Cort also figured that when he tried to remove his boots, his toes would be stuck to them and he'd be too hypothermic to care.

He hated cold weather.

Texas wasn't supposed to have winters ten degrees below freezing, which was one of the main reasons he'd chosen to relocate here rather than somewhere in his home state of Oklahoma. That and the fact that Mule Hollow was next to nothing in population made it the perfect place for a guy like him.

Or at least it would be right after he caught the prankster who'd been vandalizing his new home for the past few days. Caught him, taught him and maybe even quartered him.

Flexing his numb fingers, Cort rewrapped them

around the slender rope he'd been holding and continued his vigil. Watching, waiting and anticipating. Anticipation had all but been lost to him since the month after he'd contracted the mumps and Ramona, bags in hand, had informed him he was no longer capable of fulfilling her emotional needs or her wants in life. With the blow delivered, she had promptly marched out the door, not looking back.

The mumps. Kids had the mumps. Even now, a year later, he found it hard to believe how profoundly what was supposed to be a childhood illness had altered his life.

One day he'd had everything a man could want: a place to call his own, more than enough business to go around and a beautiful wife sharing and building a future filled with love, laughter and eventually children. Lots of children.

Then he'd contracted the mumps.

It had been a long road to acceptance, shaking the very foundation of his faith. He hadn't yet figured out what the Lord was doing, but Cort had finally managed to set what life he had left on a shaky path toward a future he hadn't planned or wanted or could ever envision being happy about.

Determined to take back some kind of control, he'd bought this secluded ranch and seven days ago he'd moved in. Here he hoped to create some semblance of a future for himself and his dog, Loser. Here he wanted to forget the anger he'd been struggling with and come to some kind of understanding about the situation forced upon him.

However, after six nights of being repeatedly vandalized, Cort found he was looking for an avenue through which to vent the fury eating away inside him.

Tonight was the night for some poor yahoo to discover exactly how humorless Cort Wells found life.

Anybody getting their jollies from unlatching stall gates and releasing thousands of dollars' worth of prize studs to tango with the mares was looking for trouble. He'd upped his stakes by ransacking Cort's feed room and tearing up his hay stash. The clown wasn't only pitiful, he was childish, because there wasn't anything any more important than alfalfa cubes inside Cort's feed room. Vandalism—pure, simple vandalism—that's what this was.

And it had Cort madder than a bull in a rodeo chute.

Trouble had seriously come knockin' at the right door.

The crunch of footsteps on gravel alerted him that he was about to entertain a visitor. He jerked to attention and welcomed the flow of warm anticipation as it surged through his chilled body. With the gentle flick of his wrist he whipped the rope in his hand to life just as the wooden door creaked, signaling his guest of honor's entrée into the barn. He heard the soft nicker of a horse and the rustle of a curious colt.

From his hiding place, Cort could hear his intruder as he shuffled over the concrete alley that ran down the center of the horse stalls. One. Two. Three steps and the clown—the chubby little clown—stepped into the circle of light from the wash bay's bug zapper. Cort hesitated, a bit surprised at the short, bulky stature of the intruder. Flicking his wrist, he heard the soft whisper as the rope sailed through the air. With an expertly tempered yank, he tightened the lasso—and had himself a culprit!

Leaping from the shadows before the first muffled cry rang out, Cort felt immediate justification when the man fell to the ground with a thud and a grunt.

That is, until *he* flopped over and turned into a *she!* A *very pregnant she!*

"Whoa!" Cort jumped back, shook his head and gaped like a fool. She didn't disappear. She didn't get any less pregnant.

Instead, frozen in the circle of light. she stared up at him with wide, warm eyes of golden fire. "Well, now, *that* was entirely uncalled for," she drawled, huffing a bit as she lay on the floor carefully touching her protruding stomach. "Do you do this sort of thing often?"

Cort was trying to scrape his lip off his boots and had absolutely no inkling of a reply. Like a buffoon, he could only stare.

She wrinkled her nose. "I know, I know. I look like a blimp floating across a full moon, but I'm not. I'm your neighbor, from down the road."

Her voice was snappy, fire and ice swirled together—and appealing as all get-out. He pictured her clowning around with small children with that voice, or whispering sweet nothings in the ear of a lonesome cowboy.

"Neighbors?" he managed at last, feeling like a stooge. Certain he looked like one.

Slowly, as if speaking to one of those toddlers he'd imagined her playing with, she nodded her red-capped head and repeated, "Neighbors. So you see, the rope really isn't necessary. As a matter of fact, you could let me go and I promise not to harm you."

That kicked Cort into gear. Things hopped out of slow motion and started to focus. He'd steer-dogged a pregnant woman! Thrown her on the ground, baby and all, and left her there.

Left her there rocking back and forth on her back, waving her arms in the air like a derailed turtle straining to flip from her back to her feet. In this case to sit up. Spurred to life, Cort grabbed her arm and started tugging.

"Thanks," she grunted. She was looking up at him with eyes full of laughing regret. "Once I'm down I'm pretty much out for the count. You know, 'help I've fallen and I can't get up.'" She chuckled at her own wit.

Cort did not. "Woman! Have you lost your mind? This is *not* a laughing matter. You could be hurt. You hit that ground like a concrete block."

"And I thank you s-o-o-o much for bringing that picture to mind," she replied. "Actually, I'm sure I look more like a beached whale doing snow angels."

Cort bit back his agreement and tugged her into a sitting position—or at least a kind of sitting position, a ninety-degree angle being a physical impossibility with her small stature and protruding stomach. The awkward position forced her to lean back into the support of his arm and compelled him to lean down over her. She was breathing hard from the exertion, and little white puffs of her warm breath mingled with his as she smiled up at him. She had a cute little pixie face dominated by sparkling eyes and dark lashes. Intelligent eyes.

"Grace in motion, aren't I?" she continued, crinkling her nose again.

Cort frowned. "Mind telling me what your name is? And what would possess you to risk your child on a night like this?"

"Lilly Tipps. And I'm padded enough that the fall didn't hurt."

Didn't hurt? This was too much for Cort. "What kind of fool is your Mr. Tipps that he lets his pregnant wife roam the countryside?"

"There is no, and has never been a Mr. Tipps."

Cort's gaze dropped to her protruding tummy and the rope resting drunkenly over it. It hit him again that he'd really lassoed a pregnant woman! His dismay must have shown, because she patted his arm in a comforting way.

"Don't look so serious," she urged. "I was trespassing on your land. You had every right to hog-tie me. It's better than being shot."

"True," he agreed with a scowl. "But we'll talk about that later. Right now we have to get you up and make certain everything is okay. Make certain that baby isn't harmed." He slipped his hands beneath his strange intruder's arms and hefted her to a standing position. Why she would be outside, heavy with child, tore at him, and the way she was leaning against him now, breathing hard, sent alarms clanging through him.

"Are you hurt?" he snapped, dropping his gaze to the top of her head where it met his chin. Her little red cap tickled his nose as she rolled her head from side to side against his chest. "What's wrong?"

"I'm all right." Her voice was muffled against his heart. "Just need to catch my breath."

Despite the intelligence he'd glimpsed in her gaze, he thought something important was missing upstairs when a pregnant woman thought nothing strange about tramping around in the middle of the night. Alone. In a storm. Unprotected.

Where was the baby's father?

Having gained her breath at last, she stepped away from the protection of his arms, and to his horror, he had to fight to let her go and drop his hands to his hips.

He watched as she adjusted her bulky coat over her bulkier body. Her face was bright, her eyes twinkling. "Thank you."

Cort couldn't tear his gaze away from her.

"I don't get much breath in here," she was saying as she ran a hand lovingly over her tummy. "That'll change in about three weeks. Although the doctor says I'll probably go past my due date."

Cort didn't see how. She looked ready to give birth any day. *Great with child* had never been a more perfect description.

"That is," she continued, "if Samantha doesn't get me killed before the end of this pregnancy. When I get my hands on her, I'm going to hog-tie *her.*"

"Who's Samantha?" Cort snapped. Multiple avenues of this scenario were rubbing his already waning good humor raw.

"Oh, I'm sorry. Sam—"

A nerve-jolting screech broke through the night air. Cort nearly jumped out of his jeans.

Half-asleep horses came alive with startled nickers and whinnies, and from inside the house he could hear his dog barking. Loser never barked. "What in the world—" Cort bit out the words, striding toward the barn door.

Lilly's laugh stopped him. "*That* is Samantha."

On one heel Cort spun toward her.

Lilly hid a smile behind her hand. "She'll be quite ornery if you changed the lock on the hay barn. Tell me it isn't so."

"Well, yes—today, as a matter of fact. The old one was broken. Some jerk keeps tearing up my hay bales."

"Samantha," Lilly mouthed softly. "She doesn't like locks on her barn." Lilly chuckled more. "She's gonna be mad."

She's gonna be mad? "Who is this Samantha person?" Cort exploded, stomping toward the door intent on finding out on his own who could make the noises coming from outside the barn.

"Watch out," she called in warning. "The hay barn was her domain."

Having reached the closed door, Cort pivoted to glare at the exasperating woman. "What? Who is Samantha?"

The words were barely out of his mouth when the barn door flew open, walloped him in the backside and sent him flying to his knees.

Lilly gasped. Cort ate dust and shot a glare over his shoulder. And there framed in the doorway stood the fattest little donkey he'd ever seen.

"Cort Wells, meet Samantha." Lilly presented her with a wave.

Cort could only stare, too startled to move. Samantha had to be the ugliest, most unassuming bag of whiskers— "A donkey!"

Lilly chuckled again and waddled to stand beside him.

"You're telling me *that* has been vandalizing my place?"

"Well, yes. Samantha used to live here and hasn't given in to nesting at my place yet."

As if to show she reigned in this domain, Samantha lifted her nose haughtily, swished her tail twice, then sashayed past them into the barn. From his stunned, all-fours position Cort had a perfect view as she swept past. He was not impressed. To say the least, Samantha was a sight—short, putty colored and instead of a smooth fat stomach she had rippling, bulging saddle bags that stretched from shoulder to rump in one roll after another. She beat all Cort had ever seen.

As he watched from his position in the dust, Samantha pranced, albeit heavily, to the feed room's closed door, wrapped her slobbery pink lips around the oval door handle, gave a twist, backed up and pulled the door open. This achieved, she stuck her nose in the air and clomped lightly inside with her tail swinging proudly.

"Well, I'll be." Cort stood, dusting off his jeans, and scratched his temple. "I'd never have believed it if I hadn't just seen it."

"Leroy, the prior owner of this ranch, raised her from a baby, bottle-fed and all. She's lived her entire twenty years here on the ranch. By the way, she thinks she's a human, or a dog at least. When she was smaller, they say she even ate bread out of her own bread box in the kitchen."

"That must be where those strange scrapes came from on that big drawer."

"Teething. She also likes you to rock her in the cedar swing next to the barn."

"Rock her. Swing? You've got to be kidding."

Samantha, on her tippy-toes, trotted out of the feed room, a green alfalfa cube sticking out of her poochy lips.

Cort jogged to the opening and groaned at the mess.

Lilly ambled over to his side. "Whew! What a nightmare. Leroy always kept her a tub of cubes open. That way she didn't make a mess, but still thought she was being sneaky."

"Just what I need. A sneaky jack—'

"Burro. Samantha prefers the less critical term to the biblically correct one. It's less demeaning to her character, if you know what I mean. And besides, she's a jenny."

Cort frowned, expressing to Lilly exactly what he thought of her terminology correction. "And *she* told you this?"

The lady had a screw loose, but at this point he'd believe anything.

"Not exactly," she said, crinkling her nose.

"Thank goodness—you had me going there."

Lilly chuckled, and he smiled at the infectious sound. Maybe she wasn't too crazy.

"She told Leroy and he told me."

Lilly's new neighbor thought she'd lost her mind. She could tell. It was written all over his face. "You really aren't as bad as everyone said." It popped out, and she could have just kicked herself for saying it. Then again, she'd never been one for holding back.

"And just what have they been saying about me?" he drawled, staring with stone-hard disapproval.

It was a shame, too, that disapproval—all those carved lines messing up his face. Boy, could he stop traffi—

The sudden tightening of her stomach broke into Lilly's runaway thoughts. Gently she rubbed the hard knot. Her back ached and suddenly the excursion took its toll. Like a glass of water being drained, she felt exhaustion overcome her. That would explain her unlikely infatuation with the new neighbor. She had learned her lesson up close and personal seven and a half months ago. All the I-told-you-so's from six generations of Tipps women would be ringing in her ears for the rest of her life for the bad choice she'd made. Yep, it was time to gather Samantha and head home to her bed before she fell over right here in the middle of Cort Wells's freezing horse barn.

However, she couldn't take that sour look one more instant. He needed to lighten up. Playing the part to perfection, she shook her head somberly. "The gossips down at Pete's Feed and Seed have been saying mean, nasty things about you. Why, you wouldn't believe what's been circulating."

His lips compressed into a thin line. "I see. And these things. You believed them?"

Lilly nodded gravely. "I was afraid to come over here tonight. Shaking in my boots. Literally." Nearly, but not exactly.

He studied her, his mouth a hardened line. The tension radiated just below the surface of his cobalt-blue eyes, and Lilly knew the moment he realized she was teasing, because his eyes mellowed ever so slightly.

"Shaking in your boots," he drawled. Arching an eyebrow, he dropped his gaze to her boots, then her stomach, then settled once again on her face. "You don't shake in your boots," he stated flatly.

Lilly laughed. "No, Cort Wells, neighbor extraordinaire, I do not shake in my boots. Nor do I listen to idle gossip with eager anticipation. The only thing I believed was that you didn't smile much and had an unfortunate habit of losing patience a little too easily." Not exactly true, but kind of.

"Which is why you stole down here to rescue Samantha from your ogre neighbor before he shot her, or worse, made glue out of her."

"Exactly," Lilly said, meeting his gaze.

For a long moment he studied her. Then, making an all-out liar of her and all the gossips, he smiled.

And Lilly, well, she shook in her boots.

Chapter Two

Standing in the center of his freezing barn, Cort stared at his kooky neighbor and felt the first smile he'd smiled in over a year spread across his face. It was an odd feeling—not unpleasant, but totally unexpected. It assured him that he needed a good, hard, swift kick in the head.

At thirty-six he was picking up speed on the down slide toward forty. His wife had left him, he couldn't father children and now he was attracted to a woman too young for him.

This was not good. Everything he'd believed in growing up he'd failed at thus far—mainly his belief that a man could be measured by his success as a good father and husband. But despite his failures, nothing altered his number one belief that a child deserved two parents.

Lilly had informed him there was no Mr. Tipps, as if it was the most natural thing in the world for a single woman to be pregnant. Obviously her view on the matter differed from his. She might be cute, but for all Cort knew, she didn't even know the name of her baby's father.

It didn't matter how good this smile cracking across his face felt—the best thing he could do for himself was get Lilly off his property. And her misbehaving donkey with her.

However, before he could do that he had to make certain she was all right. Because, despite her cheerfulness, she looked a little as if she might be hurting some in her back.

"Look," he said, blowing air into his fists to warm them. "I know you must be freezing, so why don't you come into the house, and I'll make us a pot of coffee to warm up. I'll introduce you to Loser, my dog, and then we'll get you and Samantha home." It was pure and simply an offer to warm up, nothing more.

Her eyes brightened. "Coffee," she said. "You know, I'd do fifty toe touches for a stiff cup of hot coffee— that is, *if* I could touch my toes. But I really need to get Samantha home before this storm finishes us off. The sneak, she doesn't realize what a toll her adventures play on a mammoth like me."

Cort grimaced at yet another pregnant wisecrack. To be fair, given the size of her burden, he'd bet his stash of banana Laffy Taffy that her twisted sense of humor was a cover-up. She might not care about the father of her baby, but she seemed to care deeply about her unborn child, even if she'd acted foolishly in coming out on a night like this.

As if reading his thoughts, she dropped her gaze to her stomach and placed a palm protectively on the mound where her child nestled. Cort found himself wanting to put his hand there, too, to feel life beneath his palm. A sudden violent wave of regret shook him. He'd never touch his own child that way.

He didn't like being reminded of the experiences of fatherhood that he would never have. He had come to Texas to forget them. He'd prayed that God would release him from this need, that he wouldn't be tortured forever.

Lilly moved toward the door, one hand remaining on her stomach, the other on her back, offsetting the unequal proportions.

She had moved only a couple of steps away from him when she gasped. He was beside her in a stride. "You're hurt."

Shaking her head, she paused again, exhaling slowly. "Relax. Please. I have these Braxton-Hicks all the time. You know, false labor contractions." She took another sharp breath. "My doctor assures me there isn't anything to worry about."

"Your doctor didn't know you were going to be used for roping practice when he told you not to worry."

"Forget the roping. You had every right to believe I was a thief." She gave him a quick smile. "By the way I'd like to learn that trick someday. Knowing how to use a rope like that might come in handy. Might need to catch baby Tipps. Or Samantha," she said with a wink. "Anyway, I'm just glad you didn't greet me with a gun. With an aim like yours I'd be singing praises to the good Lord right now."

Cort started to speak, but she laid one hand on his arm and touched his lips with a finger from her other hand. "There isn't anything wrong with me that my warm bed and a bit of sleep won't cure."

Cort forgot what he was about to say. She'd touched him. Big deal. She was tired and she was rambling, which he found endearing, despite himself. "How far a walk did that donkey put you through?"

She stepped away from him and started ambling along. "Oh, I parked at the end of your drive. It's not far, especially when you consider that I walk two miles every day for exercise. Poor Samantha—she doesn't mean to be so much trouble."

What had she been thinking? She'd come out in the stormy night in her condition, searching for an animal! And here he'd been thinking about how much she cared for her child. "I hope you don't make strolling around past midnight a habit," he snapped, irritated at himself as well as her.

"Scared of boogeymen, Mr. Wells?"

"Boogeymen! We're talking about being out on deserted roads alone. You're a woman. A mother-to-be, who doesn't have any business being out this late, much less alone in weather like this. You might be young, but you should have better sense."

She raised her eyebrows to where they nearly touched the edge of her red knit cap, and plunked her fists on her rounded hips. "I don't think I like your attitude."

"My attitude? My attitude! Lady, no wonder your Mr. Tipps didn't hang around." He was sputtering. He never sputtered! And he couldn't stop himself. "Anybody knows women shouldn't walk around past midnight when a storm is brewing, especially looking for a short, fat, hairy beast. And most especially when they could give birth any moment!" Cort halted his harangue to catch his breath, only to feel another tirade building as long-pent-up anger fought for release. Snatching his hat from his head, he rammed a hand through his hair and held his tongue, biting it to keep quiet.

She studied him, then shook her head slowly. "My,

my, Mr. Wells. Dare I say the gossips were correct? You are positively livid. And pink all over."

The woman was making him crazy. He'd known her all of thirty minutes and she was making him crazy. This wasn't like him.

"Samantha," she called.

Cort found himself staring as she straightened her funny red cap and lifted her chin in defiance.

Cold sobering sleet belted him in the face from the open doorway. Bewildered by his reaction, he paused to gather his wits and went to survey the dangerous conditions outside his barn.

Barely hesitating, Lilly tottered past him into the fierce night.

Unbelievable! What did she think this was? An eighty-degree, midsummer night? "Hey, do you need a keeper or what?" he yelled. He never yelled. "You can't walk in this carrying that…that baby."

Catching up to her, he grasped her arm, saving her, he was certain, from an icy catastrophe.

Ungrateful woman that she was, she promptly rewarded him with a couple of wimpy slaps on the hand. Then, yanking away from his protecting hold, she fried him with a glare.

"Would you mind? Leave me alone," she snapped above a burst of whistling wind.

In the faint glow of the light mounted above the riding pen her eyes flashed like the dancing flame of a match. It struck Cort like a burn that she sure looked cute when she was angry. She was spunky. And despite himself, he found he liked the life surrounding the little woman. He wondered at the heart behind that spunk.

"I am not an idiot, Mr. Wells," she continued,

snapping him back to reality. "The icy rain has just begun to fall. You should know it hasn't had time to freeze the ground. So would you mind dropping the 'Me Tarzan, You Jane' routine? And by the way, this is my child. Mine alone. And there never was a Mr. Tipps—and won't be if I have anything to do with it!"

Cort stared. Puffs of white-hot air wafted about Lilly like steam off the steamroller that had just flattened him.

"And thank you very much for once again proving my grannies right on all counts."

"Oh, yeah?" he managed weakly, suddenly uncentered and feeling, well...feeling alive! Lilly might be pregnant. She might be outspoken, hard to handle—the list seemed to go on and on—but after a year of walking around in a stupor, he realized Lilly Tipps had brought him back to life.

Whether he was ready or not.

"Well," she said, cutting into his spinning thoughts. Her voice was soft, deliberate. "In the words of my great-granny Shu-Shu, other than assisting in the conception of a baby, men are pert' near useless. And otherwise too bossy to worry about."

Later, watching the taillights of Lilly's truck disappearing slowly in the drizzle, Cort reminded himself that it was better this way. For a minute there he'd nearly lost his head. She'd brought him back to reality with a bang. Now he realized he didn't like her going home alone in this storm, but it wasn't his business. She was her own woman.

It didn't matter if that bit about men being useless rubbed him the wrong way. Did he care what she thought of men?

But she was something. *Something else.*

She'd tied that crazy donkey to the back of her truck and headed out at a crawl on the two-mile trip to where her home sat at the end of the lonesome road. The real estate agent had mentioned Lilly, and how she lived a fairly solitary life. They were basically secluded and cut off from everything. Except for each other. Cort had assumed she was older, and at the time he'd been happy to know his only neighbor for miles wouldn't bother him.

The real estate agent hadn't mentioned anything about her being pregnant. Or, well…kooky.

He probably hadn't wanted to scare Cort off.

Smart man. Cort would have to remember him if he ever decided to sell. Not everyone would be sharp enough to recognize a selling disadvantage in Lilly and her sidekick.

He studied the swirling sky. The full force of the storm would strike by the time she made it home. Ice pelted his face like needles. On the other hand, at the pace they were traveling the storm might have passed before they got there.

He grimaced. This was no joking matter. The weather would be a record breaker for this part of the state, for this time of year. Turning back, stiff with fatigue, nearly chilled to the bone, he headed down the drive toward the warmth of his house and the bed he'd forgotten to think about. All the while he continued to tell himself that Lilly wasn't his responsibility, a fact she'd made clear to him. Perfectly clear.

Still, as he opened the door and strode tiredly into his kitchen, he couldn't stop thinking of her. What if her truck broke? It didn't look to be in great shape. What if she slipped and fell on her way into her home? Who would help her? Samantha?

That thought spurred him to turn to the window. Loser appeared from the other room, sauntered over and with a sigh dropped his shaggy head onto the windowsill.

A perpetual sigher, Loser sighed again, drawing Cort to look down at his pitiful dog. It had been a weak moment of loneliness outside the supermarket that had been Cort's undoing. That and the cutest little brown-eyed girl trying to find a good home for the ugliest baby mutt he'd ever seen. A sap for kids, Cort had taken the pup and on a melancholy note christened the forlorn dog Loser. He shouldn't have. It hadn't been the poor pup's fault Ramona had divorced Cort and left him feeling like a loser.

Reaching down, Cort scratched him between the ears with his frozen fingers. They tingled as blood started flowing and warmth seeped back into them. Loser grunted—which was more response than Cort usually got. It was Cort's own fault. He hadn't given the dog much to aspire to by labeling him with such a lousy name. He really should change it.

But it was a name he lived up to with pride. He enjoyed hot meals, warm beds and cool breezes on sunny afternoons. He didn't like cold weather, loud noises or hairbrushes anywhere near his matted body. When he wasn't sleeping, he moped around stumbling over his own ears and looking at people's toes from beneath droopy eyelids and bushy eyebrows. The poor dog had mountains to overcome if he were ever to drag himself out of the pit of self-pity shrouding him. A state of being not unlike Cort's own.

In part, this move to west Texas had been Cort's step in the right direction. At least he was moving on with life by realizing what he couldn't have and making a new start with what he had. And most important, he had God's grace. Cort knew God's grace was sufficient to overcome the grief consuming him. But to have lost his wife and any children he'd hoped to father… He rammed a hand through his hair. He needed time to come to terms with such an incomprehensible loss. He loved the Lord, had walked every mile for the past fifteen years with a strong unfailing faith. But this wasn't something he could just move on from and pretend never happened. Lately, even trusting the Lord was a struggle. He felt as if part of him was lost forever. The Bible said there was a time to mourn and a time to dance. He wasn't ready to dance. Didn't know if he ever would be.

And he for certain didn't need a neighbor who represented everything he couldn't have. Everything he'd lost.

"We've got problems, old boy," he said to Loser. "I heard you barking. I had to think twice to realize it was you, but you knew I was in trouble up to my eyebrows. Didn't you?" Loser shifted his chin's position on the windowsill and his tail flopped halfheartedly. This, too, was more than usual. Cort reached to scratch behind Loser's ear.

"You're feeling kinda spry, aren't you? I see that tail a-wagging. You keep this perky attitude and I might have to change your name." Loser's shoulders heaved with another sigh as he returned his gaze to the storm. Cort's gaze followed the animal's and his thoughts returned to Lilly.

"I don't know why I'm worried, Loser. She wasn't. She acted as if men have leprosy or something." He glanced back at the dog. "Said we weren't worth anything if we couldn't father a child—" Loser raised his eyebrows just enough to look pityingly up at Cort. Cort frowned at the reflection he saw of himself in the dog's eyes. The reflection of the fool he'd almost been again.

"Yeah, yeah, I know," he said wearily, scrubbing his eyes and turning toward his bedroom.

"It sounded like she'd been talking to Ramona."

Chapter Three

Lilly's eyes popped open and she stared up at the ceiling. Sunlight danced across the pale yellow paint. All was quiet. No sounds of ice! Thank goodness there was no sleet this morning.

Slowly she rolled to her side, "Ohhh!" she yelped, then used her arms to rise to a sitting position, or at least a semi-sitting position. The last stages of pregnancy were a real bug-a-boo. To catch her breath she had to prop her hands on the mattress behind her just to hold herself upright because of her growing-by-the-second tummy.

She ached all over.

The run-in with her new neighbor and his little lasso had caused more soreness than she'd expected.

At least, to her great relief, the Braxton-Hicks contractions had stopped. She hadn't wanted to admit it out loud, but for a little while she'd feared she really was in labor, and she couldn't be. Not yet anyway. She had things to do. Tonight was the very first production of the Mule Hollow Cowboy Dinner Theater. And even though she had protested until she was blue in the face, she was now looking forward to being in the production.

"What a night, kiddo," she said, yawning and rubbing her tummy. "I hope you aren't sore." Talking to her baby brought a big smile to her lips. When he responded with a good hard kick to the belly button she laughed. Oh, how she loved having her little boy to talk to.

A boy. The doctor had informed her she was expecting a boy and she still couldn't believe it. A baby boy Tipps! After all these years. Wow. The grannies would most definitely be surprised.

Lilly rubbed her eyes and focused on her day. She needed to find some way to keep Samantha at home, but she didn't have the time. She had to be in town by noon. Everyone wanted her to take it easy, but she wanted to help with the last preparations for the show.

Still, she knew she couldn't be foolish again by taking chances like last night.

The weather report had predicted that the icy weather would come and go for the next week. Cort had been right about her not needing to jeopardize her baby by being out in such weather, lost burro or not. It had been only by the Lord's grace that she hadn't been harmed last night. She was determined that after the show tonight she would slow down and start acting more like how a pregnant woman ought to act.

Of course, she had to get through the show tonight. She and Samantha. They had a very important role.

Pushing herself off the bed, she padded to the bathroom and turned on the water. She had gained only thirty pounds with her pregnancy, but with her height she felt as if she was as wide as she was tall. Not that she really cared—she was having a baby!

For that wonderful cause she wouldn't care if she were, as Granny Gab would have said, as big as the broad side of a barn. *She was having a baby!*

And that was as wonderful as life could get.

Nothing else mattered. Lilly would again gladly go through everything that had led up to her pregnancy. She felt blessed.

She was blessed.

Reaching into the shower, she tested the water with her fingertip and thought about the dinner theater. Hopefully the bad weather wasn't going to hinder the program. Ever since the older ladies in the town had hatched a campaign to bring women to Mule Hollow, the town hadn't been the same. It had all started with an advertisement about lonesome cowboys looking for wives. Of course, Lilly wasn't interested in finding a husband. Everyone knew that she'd taken a chance against everything her grannies had taught her and married Jeff Turner.

And everyone knew she had no interest whatsoever in going down that road again. She had learned her lesson and learned it well.

She'd thought she could change the luck of the Tipps women. Lilly's mother, God rest her soul, had thought the same thing in her life.

Wrong.

Her mother had wound up picking the lowest of the low. And Lilly hadn't done any better. But that was water under the bridge and she had moved on.

There was only one good thing that had come of her marriage, and it was this baby she was carrying. Neither she nor her mother had been able to stop the legacy of bad choices, but as her good friend Lacy

Brown had recently pointed out to her, she had another choice to make. She could either wallow in the past or move on.

And now she was making choices for two. Another life was counting on her.

Lilly showered quickly. Normally she could hang out in the hot spray until her toes shriveled, but today she had things to do and places to be. She had to get to town and help finish decorating. Who knew a newspaper ad about lonesome cowboys needing wives would have had such an impact on her small town? Lilly combed her curly hair and chuckled at the memory of Lacy whizzing into Mule Hollow. As the first respondent, she'd been so determined in her mission. She was convinced God had called her to come to the dusty, dying town of Mule Hollow to open a hair salon, where she could witness to people as she cut their hair.

For a town left with just a handful of old-timers and a host of lonesome cowboys, the thought of families—or even of women at all—seemed an unreachable goal. But in the late 1970s after most of the town's financial support had dried up along with the oil well, many families had had to move away. Their departure had left a shell of a town that had slowly deteriorated over the decades. But now there was hope in the town. Because of the faith of three older ladies and Lacy Brown, Mule Hollow had a new spring in its step.

Lilly admired Lacy's faith. She admired her desire to follow God's plan for her life by believing He would bring women here and she would get to spruce them up to fall in love and lead them to the Lord in her hair salon, Heavenly Inspirations. In an ironic twist, it had been Lacy who'd fallen in love and was soon to marry Clint

Matlock. Theirs would be the first marriage in Mule Hollow in ten or more years.

Lilly didn't count her own marriage.

The wedding had taken place at the courthouse in the nearby town of Ranger, and the marriage had lasted just over a month. She was such a hermit that most people in Mule Hollow hadn't even known she was dating, much less gotten married! But everyone was so understanding when she explained how she'd made such a horrible mistake. And they were absolutely thrilled when they found out she would be having the first baby born in Mule Hollow in the past ten years. It was the start the town needed. And hopefully tonight's show would continue bringing new life to Mule Hollow.

Norma Sue Jenkins, Esther Mae Wilcox and Adela Ledbetter were the three ladies who'd hatched the original plan and put the ad in the papers. Tonight was the culmination of another of their ideas. Lilly would never have believed she would be participating in this cowboy dinner theater. But she was.

All because Lacy had seen her singing in the church choir.

Lilly had always loved to sing. And after Jeff left her she'd continued to go to church and sing in the choir. It was strange—even though she was hurting inside and wanted only to be alone, there was just something about being in the church singing praises to the Lord that ministered to her spirit. It didn't mean for one minute that it changed her mind about men. God was going to have to do a mighty work on her heart for her to ever look at a man as a potential husband.

Her grannies had hated men and taught her from an early age that they were useless, worthless liars, one and all. And with good reason, since they had each experienced the worst that men had to offer. And after her experience with her own loser, she'd decided to believe them. True, in the four months she'd known Lacy she'd softened to at least being able to kid around with some of the lonely cowboys who lived in Mule Hollow. Lacy had helped her see that as a Christian she needed to have a forgiving heart and not judge all men as completely useless. And by being in this presentation tonight she'd even come to like some of the guys as friends.

Friends. As Granny Gab would say, untangling grapevines took more than an hour. It wasn't until recently that Lilly had realized Gabby was talking about regaining trust. She *was* making progress, but there would never be anything more between her and another man except friendship. Her heart couldn't take it. She imagined that she was going to be like Paul in the Bible and stay single for her lifetime.

Yep, it would be just her and her baby. That was something she could trust wholeheartedly.

She finally finished getting dressed, gathered up everything she would need for the afternoon, then went to load Samantha into the trailer.

When Lacy had first approached her about letting Samantha be in the program, Lilly had been uncertain. But after a while she'd been worn down by Lacy's enthusiasm and had consented. Then, because she loved to sing, she had finally agreed to be in it also. Especially after hearing what their part would be. She couldn't resist.

She just hoped that everything went as planned. She didn't need any false labor pains tonight.

Singing while sitting on Samantha's back was going to be challenge enough.

* * *

"What do you think?" asked Molly Popp.

Lilly surveyed the room. "It looks great. Did you ever think when you moved here a few months ago that we'd be having so much fun trying to get more women to move to town?"

Molly laughed. "Honestly, I came because the entire story of what the ladies were trying to accomplish intrigued me. But I never really thought about being in on the adventure myself. This has been incredible. All these weeks of practice and planning have been great."

Lilly smiled and gently rubbed her stomach. Molly was a journalist who had a column in the Houston paper each week. After coming to the old-time fair that the town had hosted to draw women in, Molly had chosen to move right out to Mule Hollow to chronicle its progress while she started writing a book she'd been dreaming of writing.

She'd dated a few of the guys, but so far, Mr. Right hadn't come along. Unlike Lilly, Molly was still looking.

The old buildings had been transformed into part of a rustic theater. In the past few months the town had drawn together and torn out walls between two buildings, built a stage and installed woodstoves to keep the place warm for the program while still giving it the ambience of the good old days. It was a great idea.

Tonight would be the first gathering in Mule Hollow's new community center/theater.

"Lilly!" Lacy called, jogging into the room. Her short white-blond hair looked as if it had gotten caught in a blender, bouncing Meg Ryan-fashion in all different directions as she came to a jolting halt beside Lilly and Molly.

"What's up?" Lilly asked.

"I just wanted to check and see how you're doing. You feeling all right, not having any pains? Not too tired?"

"Slow down, Lacy. I'm feeling fine."

"When I asked you to do this, I wasn't thinking about how cold it was going to be. Are you sure you are up to doing your part of the show outside by the campfire?"

"My costume includes a blanket draped across my shoulders. I'll be warm enough. I love the idea of the campfire. I was over there looking at it earlier while the guys were setting up all the hay bales. It looks fantastic. Lacy, don't worry. I'll be okay. Leroy taught me to ride Samantha, and believe me, she hasn't near the energy she had way back then. The fire will give a lot of heat, and there's no drizzle on the forecast until late tonight, so I'm good to go."

Lacy grabbed her and Molly in a big hug. "Our program is going to be great tonight. I can just feel it." Lacy's face beamed with anticipation. "Yep, yep, yep, this is going to be good."

Lilly had come a long way in the past three months. She was still a loner, but she was taking steps to overcome her past.

Lacy had given her the encouragement she needed to start letting people into her life. They didn't crowd her. They recognized that she needed her space, and they gave it to her.

"Okay, it's time to get dressed," Lacy said. "I see Adela and Esther Mae coming up the street, so they'll be ready to start taking tickets as the ladies arrive."

Lilly and Molly followed Lacy into the back, where their costumes were hanging. Lilly's part wasn't until after the dinner, so she would help with waiting tables during the play, something they'd all tried to stop her from doing, but she'd insisted. Lilly had always pushed herself and always would.

She didn't know any other way.

Cort stepped into the brightly lit building full of chatter and laughter and was met by Adela Ledbetter. She was a nice lady with a gentle elegance. Her bright blue eyes set against stark white hair sparkled with welcome.

"Hello again," she said as he removed his hat and looked warily around the crowded room. "I'm so glad you decided to join us. When I invited you the other day in town I wasn't sure you would accept the invitation."

"To tell you the truth, ma'am, I didn't know I was coming until an hour ago." Cort stroked the rim of his hat and glanced around the full room again. There were women everywhere—which had him backtracking on his decision to come. What had he been thinking?

Ms. Ledbetter placed a hand on his arm and smiled up at him. "God inspired you to come, because He knew you needed to be a part of this. You're going to get a blessing."

Cort looked down, about to deny that God had anything to do with his decision, but she was looking at him with such certainty and wisdom it made him keep silent.

"Well, well, well…what do we have here?" Norma Sue Jenkins said, coming to a halt in front of him like a steamroller hitting a brick wall. She had on a pair of overalls stuffed into rubber boots and a straw hat on her head with a red bandanna wrapped around it as a hatband.

Cort had run into Norma Sue a couple of times at the feed store in the few days since his arrival in town. Both times she'd tried to start up a conversation with him, but he'd been blunt and unresponsive to her friendly overtures. Now he felt about as low as the dirt on the bottom of his boots. She beamed up at him with a genuine smile of welcome that split across her round face from ear to ear.

"Glad you could make it, son. We need all the draw we can get."

"Draw?" Cort asked.

"You know, reasons for making some of these women want to move to our town."

"Now, Norma," Ms. Ledbetter said calmly. "Cort is new in town and he doesn't fully understand the importance of our endeavor."

"Well, that will soon change. Every cowboy needs a wife. You follow me and I'll put you in a good spot between two nice ladies."

"Ms. Led—" he started to say, but she patted him on the back.

"It's Adela to my friends. Don't let Norma scare you."

"Ma'am, I just came to see the show. To see what the town has been up to." He looked around the room skeptically. "Couldn't you sit me somewhere out of the way?"

Norma Sue hooted with laughter, then grabbed his arm and practically dragged him to a table full of women. Grudgingly, Cort found himself sitting between two women who immediately started firing questions at him that he didn't want to answer. He was trying to figure a way to get up and go home when his eye caught his neighbor walking out from a room at the back of the building.

In keeping with the hillbilly theme, she also had on overalls, and her hair was split down the middle and tied into two bushy tails on each side of her head.

She was cute.

In her hand she carried a large pitcher of tea. He couldn't believe it—the woman was waiting tables! Didn't she know she was pregnant?

What else would she do to endanger her baby? The woman was obviously a glutton for punishment. Weren't women as far along as she was in their pregnancy supposed to be sitting down most of the day with their feet propped up? And here she was walking around as if everything was normal.

He watched her move among the crowd. She seemed more reserved than she'd been when he'd accosted her in his barn. She smiled and nodded and poured tea. But she wasn't sassy and talkative as she'd been in his barn. He wondered if she was tired.

She'd almost made it to his table before she saw him. When she did, she plunked a hand to her hip. At first he thought she was going to turn and walk away. He had gotten a bit overbearing the night before. But with good reason.

"I see you made it through the night," he said, deciding he'd start the conversation if she wouldn't. He hoped she was feeling better.

Her features softened. "Yes, we made it. I should say thank you—"

"Not necessarily. I'm the one who threw you on the ground. Remember?"

"What?" the two women beside him both gasped.

"Threw her on the ground!" one exclaimed.

"No, the lasso was a good idea," Lilly said hastily, her eyes skittering to the ladies then back to him. "Like I said last night, you might need to teach me to use one. You never know when one might come in handy."

She smiled then, and Cort remembered why he'd thought of her all day. That smile was the prettiest he'd ever seen, but it was something about her eyes that drew him, something in them that said back off. As if she was used to being alone, as if she expected the very worst from people…or men.

The lights dimmed, cutting off his thoughts as a group of people moved out onto the stage. Lilly quickly filled tea glasses and moved out of the way. Cort decided it was just as well. He hadn't come here tonight to think about the things he liked about his neighbor or the things about her that made him curious about her. He'd come to…well, he wasn't certain why he'd come tonight. He'd just felt compelled to check it out.

Chapter Four

Lilly sat on Samantha's back and waited in the shadows. The dinner had been a big success. The cowboys had served up hot bowls of spicy chili and she'd watched the show from the back of the room. Everyone was laughing and having a good time. Lacy had a great cast. She had cowboys who'd never stood in front of a crowd before, singing songs and reciting cowboy poetry as if they'd been doing it all their lives.

There were comical hillbilly skits, featuring Lacy, Esther Mae and her husband, Hank. They had people nearly crying they were laughing so hard. Esther wore a moth-eaten, pea-green housecoat that looked a hundred years old, her hair was half in, half out of pink curlers and she was carrying a flyswatter that she would swat Hank with every so often during his droll portrayal as a couch-potato husband. Lilly laughed thinking about Esther grinning at the audience every time she wanted a laugh. She had blacked out one of her front teeth, and she'd give this big grin that exposed the gap, then she'd swat Hank for an added laugh.

Lacy got hoots of laughter on her own playing their less-than-intelligent, husband-hunting daughter. They worked well together—they were having as much fun doing the skit as everyone was having watching them.

Then there was Clint, Lacy's real-life fiancé, who also played her newfound love in the skit. It almost gave Lilly hope watching them singing love songs together—they couldn't carry a tune in a bucket, but that made it all the more humorous.

"You're next, Lilly. Hang on, now."

Lilly was roused from her thoughts and looked down from where she sat on Samantha's back. Bob Jacobs smiled up at her. Since starting the play, they had become good friends. He had the cutest dimples and a friendly but shy way about him. He would make someone—not her—a great husband. Maybe tonight's show could help out with that.

"We don't want anything happening to you tonight," he added, checking the saddle to make certain it was tight. "Okay, hold on. I'll take care of you." He winked up at her.

Lilly smiled and settled herself securely on the side-saddle, thankful that it helped her proportions angle more comfortably into the ride. She was a great rider; she'd been taught by the best. Leroy, the only man she'd ever been around much during her life, had taught her and she had no fear of a mishap. Everybody else was a bit apprehensive, but she'd be okay. Samantha would never intentionally do anything to harm her. Goodness, if Lilly hadn't been pregnant she'd have been riding bareback.

"Lead the way, Bob. Good luck—I mean break a leg." He grinned at her traditional theater jargon, pulled his costume hood over his head and took on the role of Joseph leading Mary toward Bethlehem.

The production inside had been in fun, but around the campfire were cameos of different Bible stories. Hers was a retelling of Jesus' birth.

"Let's go, Samantha," she said, patting the little burro on the neck as she started taking slow cautious steps. She knew it was Sam's nature to prance, but with Lilly on her back, the little dear was doing her bit to protect Lilly. It seemed to Lilly that Samantha understood the serious part they were playing in the drama. Samantha perked her long ears up and slapped her tail as if to say here we go, and then she followed Bob into the circle of light made by the large campfire.

In the crowd Lilly could see the faces of women and some children. Cowboys were interspersed in the gathering also. Friends had been made tonight by many of the singles, and Lilly was glad for them. The more social things that the town could host, the more likely it would grow. She was glad to be a part in helping with that goal.

Whether she believed there was any love out there for her or not.

Cort was standing to the side of the campfire. Roy Don, one of the few men Cort had met at the feed store and had actually let himself converse with, was playing the part of an old cowboy telling stories from the Bible. With each story he told someone dressed as that character stepped up and sang a song. It was entertaining and creative. Cort had to give them credit—the town had talent. Everyone gathered around the campfire seemed to really enjoy it. It was a nice touch of old-time authenticity to it and a great ending to a great night.

Despite his misgivings, he'd enjoyed the evening. He'd laughed so hard his gut was sore.

He surveyed the setup. They'd placed about forty hay bales around the camp for seating and had more stacked around with cowboy decorations hanging off them. He'd never seen so many lassos, lanterns, hay bales and hitching posts.

Someone had put in many hours of decorating for this night. When they decided to do something, they went all out.

Leaning against a porch post, Cort surveyed the crowd. He hadn't seen his neighbor for a little while. To his relief she hadn't done anything else after pouring the tea. The cowboys who weren't in the play did all the serving of the food. Cort had relaxed. He didn't know why he worried so much about the little sable-haired mother-to-be, but he did. Maybe the foolishness of the night before hadn't been out of negligence toward her baby, but out of misguided loyalty toward her donkey.

When he saw her being led out into the circle of light balanced on Samantha's back, he took back every nice thing he'd just been thinking.

The woman was due anytime, and she was sitting high up on a donkey. He hung his head in disgust.

It was all he could do not to stomp up there and lift her off her precarious perch. The fool woman ought to have her head examined. But when she started singing, he froze.

Her voice carried out across the crowd with a haunting melody. Cort took a step off the porch, drawn toward the sweet music.

It was a beautiful song. A beautiful voice.

It was a gentle whispery sound that floated over the audience in a poignant melody that pulled Cort to attention and took him on a journey of wonder. She sang of a mother, unsure of her future, uncertain of what God had in store for the child she carried, afraid of not raising him right, but believing that God had a plan and knowing she had two choices—trust God or turn Him away.

The song reminded Cort of how vulnerable Mary must have been back then. A mother-to-be with an unbelievable story. It amazed him how Lilly was able to incorporate all the angst and hope into one song. And all the while she sang, Samantha stood still, doing her part as the donkey that carried the special burden of God's Son and His mother into Bethlehem to bring hope to all people.

It was a stirring cameo. Of all the wonderful things Cort had seen during the evening, this was the most important and most touching. This one scene brought the essence of life into perspective.

He now understood the significance of the scene to Lilly. Why she might have thought it vital enough to sit on the burro's back as near term as she was. She did look at ease sitting there, even if she had to accommodate the roundness of her middle by leaning back. And Samantha had been perfect.

He was about to eat crow and relax when out of the corner of his eye he saw a kid toss something black into the fire.

Bang! Bang, bang!

Yells and screams broke out within seconds of the eruption of the firecrackers. When the explosions burst suddenly in rapid succession Samantha whirled and backed into the campfire flame, even with the grip Bob had on the lead rope.

Cort had already started forward to help Lilly when the fringe on Samantha's tail caught fire.

The old girl yanked her head up in panic, kicked her hind legs out and bolted. Terror filled her wide eyes.

Cort snatched the nearest lasso off a hitching post and jumped into the path of the frenzied animal. Lilly was hanging on to the sidesaddle, but had nothing with which to control Samantha. Cort could almost imagine the panic she must be feeling. Bob had been knocked down in the fray and was trailing them, but losing ground.

The flames on Samantha's tail were blazing. Cort knew he had to stop her before the fire reached her flesh and real pain began.

With a flick of his wrist Cort had the lasso spinning. He took a firm stance and let it fly just as Samantha whirled toward the alley and open range. Cort prayed his aim was true, and was rewarded when the cord settled over her head. He held on as the rope tightened.

Someone reached Samantha and threw a blanket over her tail to smother the fire just as Cort drew the rope taut. Lilly, miraculously, had managed to hold on during the fiasco.

Everything had happened within a few short moments, and now everyone was in motion, putting out the fire and trying to get Lilly off the donkey. Cort wrestled through the throng, reached up and lifted her from the burro's back.

"Are you okay?"

Lilly laughed.

Laughed!

Her eyes were sparkling, dancing. "You are really good with that rope. Wow! Samantha? How's Samantha? Man, that was some ride."

What? Did the woman have no sense? No shame? Once more she'd endangered her child. Her defenseless little baby who might, and then again might not, be born into this world.

"That donkey is fine," he growled. "You're the one who needs her head examined. The fire only singed her tail. What were you thinking?"

Everyone around them went silent. The only sound was the cold wind whistling around the edge of the buildings. Cort didn't care. Why, all of them were foolish if they saw nothing wrong with Lilly riding that stinkin' donkey.

"I was thinking I had it under control. I was thinking that I knew how to ride—"

"Well, that was a wrong assumption."

"Now, wait just a minute," Bob interjected from where he was again holding Samantha's lead rope. This time he had it wrapped around his hand tightly. "I'm the one to blame here. I was supposed to control Samantha. If you're going to tear someone up, then tear into me."

He looked remorseful standing there. And he should. He'd made a grave mistake. Cort scanned the group of men and couldn't figure out why none of them had kept Lilly from getting on that donkey's back.

"Lilly, I'm sorry," Bob continued. "That song does it to me every time. I just forget about everything when you sing it, and I wasn't holding on securely."

"Bob, I'm a big girl." She patted his arm. "And I can take care of myself on a donkey or a horse's back. So relax." She lifted her chin and locked eyes with Cort.

Cort seriously doubted that the statement had merit. "Control? You were barely hanging on to Samantha's saddle horn. You could be on your way to the hospital right now. You're about the most thickheaded woman I've ever met."

Lilly rammed a hand through her ringlets and took a step toward him. Steam practically spewed from her ears. Good, Cort thought with satisfaction, she was mad. Someone needed to get through to her. Needed to make her realize that what she was carrying in her womb was precious cargo. That not everyone was so lucky.

"Thickheaded? Cort Wells, you are the most high-handed, overbearing man I have ever met. Have I, in any of our bizarre encounters, given you the slightest notion that I was in need of your guidance? I don't think so."

Cort watched anger play across her beautiful pale skin…. Oh, no, you don't! He yanked his thoughts away from admiring her and back to the problem at hand. "You might not think it, but that doesn't change anything."

"Ohhh!" She glared at him and stomped her tiny foot. "This was such a good night, and now it has morphed into a bad dream. And you are—"

Lacy Brown stepped up beside Lilly, placing her hand on her arm to stop her from speaking. "Y'all 'bout ready to finish the play?"

Cort frowned and Lilly glowered at him, her flashing eyes alive with fiery indignation as Lacy proceeded to call everyone back to the campfire.

Cort figured she had a point. There was no sense in his continuing to make a scene in front of the entire town and its guests. There was, after all, no reason for him to make a scene period.

Lilly meant nothing to him.

He didn't even know the woman. Why he'd gotten it into his lame brain that he had a right to tell her what she should and shouldn't do was completely beyond him. As everyone else moved back to the campfire, he headed to his truck. He'd never been big on crowds and had had about as much fun as one man could stand in a single evening.

He needed to be out in the country where he could be alone.

Cort hadn't been sure why he'd come to town, but Adela had been way off the mark when she'd said he was going to get a blessing from it.

Blessing? Cort couldn't remember the last time God had granted him one of those.

Chapter Five

Lilly needed a shower. She needed to feel the hot water pelting the fog from her brain and the soreness from her muscles. She hurt everywhere. Okay, she'd been foolish and reckless and was paying for it. Thankfully, her baby wasn't. He seemed fine, kicking and moving and generally having a grand time this morning.

A rap on her back door startled her. Company? At this hour? Her fingers froze in shock on the top button of her flannel pajama top. When was the last time she'd had someone rapping on her door?

Forever.

The knocking grew to a pounding, so she turned the shower off and waddled as fast as her short legs would carry her down the long hallway lined with pictures of her many generations of Tipps women.

"Hey, Grannies, someone is knocking at my door." Company was a very abnormal occurrence—still, Lilly wasn't sure that made her talking to photos any less pathetic. Maybe she should get out more. She reminded herself that she had been helping out with the play a couple of nights a week for the past month. But now that the play was over, she had nowhere to go.

That was okay. She obviously had no people skills. She'd behaved shoddily last night. It had been such a wonderful night, and then she'd allowed Satan a hold over her and run her neighbor off with her sharp tongue.

All night she hadn't been able to get the memory of Cort stomping away in anger out of her mind. She'd driven him away, and he'd just been trying to help her.

True, he was bossy, and had a bad way with words. But so did she, and she hadn't had control of Samantha. Her adrenaline had simply been pumping from the excitement, and she'd said some pretty silly things. She needed to apologize to Cort. They were neighbors, for crying out loud. Why couldn't they get along? They were the only ones around for miles.

A quick look in the mirror by the door had her slapping a hand over her mouth.

"Eeks!" It was a bad, bad thing to wake up looking like Shirley Temple gone wrong. *Way wrong.* She really needed that shower.

"I hope whoever is on the other side of this door has a good heart," she muttered, then straightened her back and lifted her chin. Who cares what I look like, anyway? she thought.

Cort, standing on her porch, immediately made a mockery of that thought. She ran a hesitant hand through her tangled hair, but the moment his stone-cold gaze met hers she knew it was hopeless. His eyes flickered to her curls, registered alarm or hysteria—two very close expressions—then flicked back to her face. To his credit he controlled his laughter.

That is, if the man had any laughter. Just as he'd

looked last night, he looked about as friendly as a por-
cupine. Granny Gab would say he looked as if he'd
swallowed a pickle with a hook in it.

"I believe I have something that belongs to you," he
drawled, none too happily holding up the end of a lead
rope. A lead rope attached to—

"Samantha!" Lilly exclaimed, stepping onto the
porch. "You didn't? Not again."

"What's new?" Exasperation edged his voice, and
Lilly couldn't blame him.

"I found her stuffing her face in the alfalfa bin
when I went out to ride this morning. Don't you feed
this animal?"

"I am so sorr—*yes,* I feed the little pig. Leroy
spoiled her so much that I don't know what I'm going
to do with her." Lilly wrapped her arms about her
tummy and shivered in the icy morning air. After the
show ended last night, the sleet had rolled in again. The
sun had come out for the morning, but the wind was
still bitter.

Despite his obvious irritation and dislike for her, Cort
motioned toward the doorway and remained true to his
bad habit of telling her what to do. "You'd better get back
inside. I'll tend to Samantha. You tend to your baby."

If she hadn't been feeling guilty about her own bad
behavior, and if she hadn't been so cold, she might have
rebuked him. Instead she backed toward the door. The
last thing she wanted was the irritating man having to
take care of her business, but she was too chilled to
protest. And he was right. She didn't need to risk falling.

"Her stall is the second one in the barn. Surely she
has to be exhausted from all her scavenging. I think
she'll stay put for at least a little while."

Cort didn't look as if he agreed. He stomped off the porch and strode toward the barn with long, determined steps.

He hadn't gotten far when he slipped on a patch of ice. His legs went flying from beneath him and he splattered right at Samantha's feet.

"Oh!" Lilly gasped, starting toward him.

"Stay right where you are!" Cort's harsh shout stopped her with one foot hovering between the inside and the outside. "Don't even think about coming off that porch." Slowly sitting up, he rubbed the back of his head and glared at Samantha.

His hat had flown off and his dark hair fell across his forehead in a thick, shiny swath. It wasn't exactly the time to notice, but he had really nice hair, despite his grumpy disposition.

"This little beast is going to get one of us killed. The sun's made all this ice very slick, so stay put."

Nice hair or not, he really didn't need to repeat himself. Lilly had already complied with his demands— only because she was afraid she would end up on the ground beside him if she didn't. Her bones were aching from the last two nights' escapades. She didn't need any more strenuous activity.

She watched him straighten his six-foot bossy frame. Cort was an extremely attractive man. Even if he was difficult.

The grannies would not have been pleased to know she continued to notice such a thing. Lilly nibbled on her lip. Of course, it hadn't helped that she'd thought about his smile off and on for two days. But most of all she'd thought about his frown.

What would make a man frown so much? It was a

question she was really curious about. There was a part of her that wanted to make him smile.

Poor guy—meetings with her had certainly not given him anything whatsoever to smile about. Except that once.

"You do know that it's a proven fact that if you were having a bad day, a laugh or even just a smile would improve your disposition." Now, why in the world had she said that? He replied with the same question when he nailed her with a glare. She wasn't doing his disposition any good. Things had gone quickly from bad to worse.

And it didn't improve when in the next instant, to Lilly's horror, Samantha picked Cort's hat up off the icy ground and started chewing!

Lilly closed her eyes and groaned, "Oh, Samantha, how could you?"

When it came to being around his new neighbor, Cort had endured about as much humiliation as one man could stand. Had it not been for Samantha nosing around his barn, this would have been the last place he'd have come this morning.

After last night, he hadn't cared if he ever saw Lilly again. She and her donkey had become thorns in his side.

Forget feeling alive again. He wasn't sure he liked the cost.

Right now he was cold and wet, and his attitude toward Lilly or Samantha wasn't improving. Both seemed to have a distaste for him. His hat, on the other hand, was an altogether different story.

The hairy bag of bones was staring down at him with doe-brown eyes while mutilating his favorite Stetson with her slobbery mouth.

Something about this picture just wasn't right.

Carefully he stood up. Not wanting to sprawl on the ground again, he hid his pride, made like a little old man and took his time.

"Gimme that," he growled once he was on his feet. He snatched at the hat—or attempted to snatch it—but the cantankerous donkey bit down on the brim and held on as if she had lockjaw.

That did it. Cort's patience snapped. Grasping the brim of the hat, he yanked hard, but Samantha, the little prankster, was having none of it. She wagged her head from side to side and started backing up in a tug-of-war.

"Hey, you little beast! Let go of that."

"Samantha." Lilly whooped with laughter from the doorway.

Cort shot her a sharp look. So much for his pride. It was on the line and she was laughing.

"Samantha needs obedience school," he snapped. "What is up with this donk—" He nearly fell over when Sam let go of the hat abruptly and trotted off, fried tail swishing to and fro in a singed frizzy ball.

Cort grunted, slammed his hat onto his head and carefully followed Samantha to where she stood looking at him like an expectant puppy. In all his years dealing with horses, he'd never come across anything quite like Samantha. She was almost human.

"Cort, leave her there and come in. You're cold and wet and I'm so sorry about all of this. Please." She hesitated, replacing the edge in her voice with sincerity. "Please let me make you some coffee. Believe me, Samantha isn't going anywhere right now. And I think we need to start over. What do you say?"

Thawing to the invitation, Cort turned toward Lilly

and raised an eyebrow. "How do you know she isn't going anywhere?"

Lilly laughed. "She's like Curious George. She'll have her nose plastered to the window the minute you enter this house. The busybody wants to be in the know about everything."

Coffee did sound good. And the donkey was home. And Lilly was smiling, offering coffee…and they were neighbors. They needed to be able to get along. So why was he standing out in the cold when he could be inside with a cup of hot java?

Looking into the laughing eyes of his neighbor, he could think of a lot of reasons.

But at the moment he didn't want to list them.

Chapter Six

Lilly held the door open wide to allow Cort entry. He stepped onto the linoleum, moving just far enough inside for her to close the door, as if he wasn't certain he wanted to be there. She didn't blame him. She wasn't positive she wanted him, either, but she'd had to invite him in. It was the neighborly thing to do.

In the small space of the entry hall his stature was magnified, making her lack of height all the more obvious. Standing there, he looked uncomfortable, with his rumpled hat in hand, wet jeans and heavy work jacket.

"Oh, here!" Lilly said quickly, reaching for his hat. "Let me take that. Oh, your poor hat. I'm so sorry about the chewing. Why don't you take off your coat and I'll throw it in the dryer while we have that coffee I mentioned."

Boy, could she use it, too. She really didn't know what had gotten into her. Men didn't usually make her nervous. But then, she hadn't ever been as rude to a man as she'd been to Cort.

Of course, no man had ever made her as mad as he had, either.

But none of that explained why her heart was pounding so erratically or why her brain had gone west. Or south—? Ugh! She needed some coffee. And some taffy wouldn't hurt, either.

"You really don't have to dry my jacket," he said, stripping off the damp coat. "It's waterproof. It looks wet on the outside, but I'm dry except for my jeans."

Lilly took the jacket from him and studied it. Sure enough, it was dry inside. Cort's spicy scent rose from the coat and tickled her senses.... *Nope, none of that.* "I'll just hang it up here, then," she said, hooking the coat and hat on the rack beside the door. She caught a glimpse of herself in the mirror as she did, and cringed. She could just hear Granny Gab exclaiming, "Child-a-mine, you look like something the cat dragged in."

Yeah, well, so be it. Pushing aside her pride, Lilly moved through the doorway into the kitchen. "Come on in," she called over her shoulder.

She pressed the button on the coffeepot. She always prepared the pot the night before so that it was a quick thing to have her morning caffeine fix. She'd tried the decaf and had high hopes that it would grow on her, but so far it was a no-go. Therefore for the baby's sake she allowed herself only one cup of regular coffee in the morning.

"Why don't you stand over there?" She waved a hand toward the wall heater and avoided eye contact with Cort as she popped the top off the canister next to the icebox and grabbed a couple of pieces of taffy—the way she was feeling, she held back from tucking the whole can under her arm and running away to scarf it down. "You can dry out those jeans while I go do something about this monster on my head." Not waiting to hear him agree or disagree, she hurried out of the room and down the hallway.

At least, she tried to hurry. Waddling gave a person little room for speed no matter what the emergency. There was no way she could appear pleasant knowing she looked the way she did. Man or no man, no one should have to endure what she'd seen in the mirror.

Cort watched as Lilly disappeared down the hall. She was a cute little thing, with her hair all crazy. Those curls looked alive the way they stood out all over her head. He'd noticed immediately that they bounced with her every step. He'd also noticed the way they curled around her pixie face and how the darkness of the curls contrasted with her pale skin and caused her golden eyes to warm like honey in the morning sunlight. But there was something more than the way she looked that had him following her with his eyes. There was a wariness about her. She was a paradox. At times he glimpsed a take-charge kind of bravado and at other times he glimpsed something almost sad hidden in her eyes—it seemed that she, too, had a past. A past that—like his—had left scars. He wondered how deep hers ran.

What was he thinking?

He didn't like the effect his neighbor had on him. He was here to get his life back on track. And that had nothing to do with a kooky gal about to have a baby. Walking over to the wall heater, he waited for Lilly to return while he warmed his back and closed down his newfound need for companionship.

Companionship that could go nowhere for a man like him.

Feeling like a bear in a trap, he took in his surroundings. Lilly's home reminded him of his grandmother's house. The kitchen was large and open with white painted cabinets and green Formica countertops. The green-and-white-checked curtains in the window had red roosters lined up across the bottom. In the corner of the kitchen beside the gas stove there was a large whitewashed cupboard with chicken wire insets in front of a mass of brightly colored dishes. In the center of the room was a long wide island, and Cort imagined many meals having been prepared there. It was a farmhouse kitchen—warm, useful and inviting.

A noise at the window beside the breakfast table drew his attention. Samantha stood just outside the pane with her damp nose plastered to the glass, two huge circles of fog highlighting each nostril as she breathed hot and heavy against the glass. That was truly one strange little burro. As he watched, Samantha turned her head sideways and plastered one eyeball against the glass, as if trying to see at a better angle. Her eyelashes made stripes in the fog as she batted them against the glass.

"She's a nosy girl," Lilly said, startling him.

He turned at her comment. In a matter of seconds it seemed she had tamed her hair with something that smelled good. She had changed into a pair of overalls and a bright pink top. She looked—what did it matter how she looked? Cort tore his gaze away from Lilly and focused on the hairy girl in the window.

"Nosy. You can say that again," he agreed. "I don't think I've ever seen anything quite like your Samantha."

Lilly grabbed two mugs from the cabinet and poured coffee into them.

Cort was in need of the rich-smelling brew. His brain

was fogged up more than all the steam streaming out of Samantha's nose onto the windowpane.

"Cream or sugar?" Lilly asked with a bright smile. It was obvious that she was trying to be pleasant to him. He needed to do the same.

"Just black, thank you."

She pushed one cup toward him, then counted out three heaping teaspoons of sugar into the other cup. Walking over, Cort picked up his cup and watched as she proceeded to dump just as much if not more creamer into hers, then pick up her spoon and begin to stir.

And stir.

And stir.

She grinned. "I stir exactly twenty-seven times. Granny Bunches always said that twenty-six was too little and twenty-eight was too much. Twenty-seven was the magic number that caused the coffee's flavor to bloom to its full potential."

Cort lifted an eyebrow and watched Lilly place the cup to her mouth, close her eyes and sip.

"Mmm, mmm, good. Granny Bunches sure told the truth."

The woman could sell coffee to millions if she were on TV. Watching her savor the aroma before she took a sip had Cort wanting to trade his cup in and have what she was having. Normally he never added cream or sugar to his coffee. His only weakness was for taffy, but that was it on the sweet stuff. He could never say no to taffy.

She laughed, popping her eyes open and winking at him. "My granny was full of weird little top secret things like that. She shared them with me throughout my childhood." She rattled off a few more things about her grannies, tilting her head to the side and chuckling as she recalled them. There was a softness in her voice and a twinkle in her eye at the remembrance. Then she frowned. "Of course, not all they taught me was cute or funny. Granny Shu-Shu would be madder than a wet hen if she knew your kind was standing in her kitchen."

Cort took a sip of his hot coffee and tried not to choke on the steaming liquid when Lilly lifted her eyes to meet his and winked at him again. He could almost hear Granny Shu-Shu telling him he was worthless.

"Are you okay?" she asked, shuffling over and peering up at him.

"Fine. I'm fine." He bit out the words while the hot liquid burned a layer out of his stomach before fizzling out.

"Granny Gab would say take smaller sips." She was beaming and wagging a finger at him playfully. The flicker of a frown was gone, replaced by the lighthearted girl who seemed almost determined to show him that she wasn't hard to get along with.

Cort scowled down at the little pixie smiling up at him. She had a way about her. "You always like this?"

She backed away, one hand resting beneath her tummy as if supporting it. "Like what?" Picking up her cup, she ambled over and sat at the table next to the batting eyeball of Samantha. She thumped the windowpane with her fingers, making Samantha turn her damp nose and smudge the glass.

"Perky." The word jumped out of him. Yeah, *perky,* that was the word to describe Lilly Tipps. Waddling or not, the woman was perky personified.

He watched her lift her feet one at a time and place them with a thud on the chair she'd scooted out in front of her. She had on striped socks that looked like gloves for the toes.

"I wouldn't call this perky. I feel like I'm gonna blow any moment now." Sighing, she took another sip and wiggled her toes. "These legs of mine feel about as heavy as—oh, never mind. Yes, I usually have a lot of energy. But that's enough about me. I truly am sorry for all the trouble Samantha is causing you. And about my rude behavior last night. I didn't have everything under control. I just get excited about weird things sometimes. I am so grateful you caught Samantha before the fire reached her skin. Thank you."

Cort studied Lilly. "You're welcome," he said, noticing how she looked tired around the eyes. He couldn't help wondering about those false labor pains she'd been having that first night in his barn. He might have come to Mule Hollow seeking solitude, but there was no way he could ignore the fact that his neighbor looked as if she needed a little bit of help.

Even if all those grannies she was so fond of quoting had filled her mind with a bunch of hogwash about men. He also kept reminding himself that everything she did was her business. It didn't matter if he agreed or disagreed.

"Don't worry about Samantha. It looks like she's been wandering for a long time. I'll figure something out," he said. Being alone and pregnant, the poor woman had enough to worry about without having to fret over Samantha bothering him. "Her visiting me isn't that big of a deal. If it weren't for my show stock it wouldn't matter at all."

"I understand completely," she said with a sigh. "I know I could lock her in. And I should."

She rubbed an earring between her thumb and forefinger, worry in her eyes. Again it hit Cort that she had a lot on her plate. Where was her husband? The question had bothered him ever since she'd told him there was no Mr. Tipps. And never would be. So if there never was, then what had happened to her? With her distaste for men in general he didn't know what to think.

What does it matter? It's none of your business, he thought.

Yeah, but Samantha was one thing he could help her with.

Setting his cup on the counter, he reached for his jacket. "Leave her be and I'll figure out something over on my end—that is, if you don't go out looking for her in the middle of the night again." He pinned hard eyes on Lilly, hoping she'd heed his warning for the sake of her baby.

She looked almost as if she had a jaunty reply ready for him, but then surprised him with one of those smiles that socked him in the gut despite his need to dodge the blow.

"I can do that," she said. "I guess you need to get home?"

"I've got horses to exercise and stalls to clean, and daylight's burning," he grunted, forcing himself not to ask for another cup of coffee. "The sun's not going to last long, you know. That ice is going to start laying down again after lunch. You need anything?" He had to ask. His conscience would allow nothing less of him.

She shook her head. "Nope, thanks. I'm fine."

Nodding, he stepped out the door. The blast of cold had him wishing for the warmth of Lilly's kitchen, but his better sense told him to go home and stay there.

Lilly might not think highly of men, but that didn't keep him from wondering just why exactly that was. What could have happened to turn all the Tipps women against men?

* * *

Lilly watched Cort walk carefully out to his big truck and drive away. The man was not a grinch…not exactly. She'd caught that hard look he'd given her when he'd asked if she could hold herself back from going out in the night in search of Samantha. Her first reaction had been to tell him that it wasn't any of his business what she did, but something had passed across his tough expression, something in his eyes, in the softening of his voice—longing, regret…something. Whatever it was, it had touched Lilly. It had reached in deep and wound around a dark place in her heart that she had locked away and was determined to keep locked…and yet she'd responded to it by keeping her mouth shut.

The grannies wouldn't have liked it, but what was done was done. Instead she'd smiled, nodded and told him she could refrain from wandering around at night taking care of Samantha, for her baby's sake.

Lilly was all her baby had. Her grannies were gone. One at a time they'd passed on into eternity, leaving her alone with a bunch of heartfelt advice. And memories. So many memories. When she thought of Granny Shu-Shu and Granny Gab she pictured vinegar mixed with sugar. So much hurt and bitterness filled their lives. Both had been hurt by the men they'd loved. Their pain also ran through Lilly's veins, put there like poison. Granny Bunches had tried to turn aside the bitterness, to show Lilly that there were other opinions in the world. But after Lilly experienced her own rejection, her heart had hardened. She was working on expelling the past, on moving forward. Some days were good. Some days weren't.

Cort Wells confused her. He seemed to have his own

pain, or memories to fight. Maybe that was why she felt this odd connection with him.

Lilly pushed herself out of the chair. She needed to do her chores for the day and then do some work on the catalog. There was always a fence that needed fixing. But the weather was too bad for that. Tomorrow she'd check the fence down by the creek that connected to Cort's place. She didn't want Tiny, her bull, getting over on his property. Cort had enough problems with Samantha trotting over there whenever she pleased. Lilly decided to catch up on her laundry first—anything to get rid of the disturbing internal need she kept feeling to see that smile return to her neighbor's lips.

Chapter Seven

Lilly stretched. She was glad she'd decided to remain indoors. She'd plenty to do to fill up her day. Running a small cattle operation needed supplemental income. Lilly had been configuring a cattle sales catalog for a cattle company out of Ranger for the past five years. She scanned the pictures into the computer and made certain all the pertinent information on each animal was correct, then sent it to the printer for her client. It was a good business and it helped her continue living on the ranch by providing the extra income she needed to survive on the land that had been in her family for generations.

It also meant endless hours sitting at her computer staring at the screen long after most people had the good sense to go to bed. But the job had to be done.

Glancing around the house, Lilly sighed. It was quitting time. She wouldn't get any more done tonight. It had been a long day and was way past time for bed. Her steps were heavy as she padded into the rear entrance hall to lock the door. She paused to rub her throbbing back. Whew, maybe heat would help. Forgetting to lock the door, she decided to grab the heating pad from the pantry.

Her back was throbbing like a jackhammer.

Five hours sitting in front of the computer screen was entirely too much. But she had a deadline and it couldn't be helped. Commitment was something she took very seriously. And she needed the money. She had a baby coming she needed to support. Alone.

Jeff Turner intruded upon her weary mind. She tried not ever to think about her ex-husband. His lack of commitment to anything, especially her and their baby, always stabbed her with regret. It ripped at her determination to move forward and forget about the things she couldn't change.

Regret. Lilly forced it from her mind and heart. It wasn't always an easy task.

There had been a few very hard weeks in a marriage that fell apart as quickly as it had begun. A marriage that hadn't really been a marriage, but more of a rebellion.

Funny, optimistic Lacy Brown had helped Lilly gain perspective on trying to allow God's timing and His will to take precedence over her past. Lacy had impressed Lilly with her brute determination to do God's will. The joy that animated Lacy was contagious, and Lilly was trying to learn to renew her mind by replacing negative thoughts with positive. "For as he thinketh in his heart, so is he." Lacy had asked her to memorize the verse from Proverbs. She found herself quoting it often.

She'd been raised by a band of grannies who had many takes on how life should be lived. Many of those ideas she was trying to rethink. It wasn't always easy, but she was determined to be a positive-thinking, active, Christian mother to her child.

Speaking of which, she remembered telling Cort that there had never been a Mr. Tipps. There hadn't been a Mr. Tipps. She'd been Mrs. Turner before returning to her maiden name, but despite the legalities of the wording, she had misled Cort. She'd have to remedy that. He needed to know that she valued family. She'd just let her mouth get carried away while she was angry—her mouth did that quite often. One of the negative things about being raised by her outspoken grannies was that two of them believed it was okay to say whatever was on their mind.

No matter whom it hurt.

Mind renewing was hard work! But with the Lord's help Lilly was determined to rid herself of some very odd ideas from a very odd upbringing.

Suddenly realizing she was standing by the icebox lost in thoughts of her past, she focused. Did she need heat for her aching back or something cold? Granny Gab was the one who'd taught her to use a bag of frozen vegetables as an ice pack. Black-eyed peas happened to be her veggie of choice.

Heat. She needed heat tonight.

A noise at the window made Lilly close the icebox and walk over to peer into the darkness. An ice-encrusted Samantha stood staring back at her.

"Samantha!"

The little mischievous dear, whose neck she often wanted to wring, would be ill if this continued. But what was she to do? Cort had been right. She couldn't keep going out in this weather.

Samantha knew where her stall was. She knew there was fresh feed and dry straw in the barn, as well as plenty of protection from all this sleet.

"Please go to bed. I can't take a chance leading you over to the barn." With a heavy heart Lilly grabbed the heating pad from the pantry, turned off the light and trudged down the hallway to her room. There was nothing she could do for Samantha right now. No amount of worrying was going to change that tonight. Her baby came first.

She was pulling the covers over her and about to turn out her lamp and settle down with the heating pad when the electricity blinked and went out.

This was not good.

Worse, Lilly thought, sitting up on the edge of the bed, pain radiated all through her lower spine and down the backs of her legs. She'd definitely worked too long today. After a few moments the lights remained off and a chill started to creep into the room.

Samantha had walked around the house and was now staring at Lilly through the lace of her curtains. Lilly felt truly sorry for the obstinate old girl. The heater was off and a touch of the coldness Samantha was enduring was settling into the house.

Lilly rose. Despite the pain, she knew she needed to start a fire. Loading her comforter into her arms and grabbing her pillow, she headed down the hall into the living room. There was already a significant feeling of ice in the air inside the house. It didn't take her long to build a roaring fire in the large fireplace.

"Thank you, Lord, for giving me a fireplace." Pulling the fireplace guard closed, she was turning to crawl onto Granny Shu-Shu's overstuffed couch when she was engulfed by pain. Red-hot explosions of agony ripped through her back, around to her abdomen and buckled her knees. She caught herself with her hands on the edge of the couch and fought to stand.

This was not Braxton-Hicks.

There was nothing false about what was happening to her.

It was time.

As Lilly concentrated through the contraction, a groan escaped her clenched lips. She held her abdomen and eased toward the phone in the kitchen. Who would she call? She wasn't ready. She was supposed to have a month to prepare.

Gasping when the pain hit full force, she made it to the kitchen and grabbed the phone.

This was too soon. Not the way it was supposed to be.

Lilly dialed 911 and put the phone to her sweaty cheek. It took a moment for the silence on the line to register.

She was in labor, in the middle of nowhere, and the phone was dead.

Zip, nada, nothing…dead.

Cort woke with a start in the faint light of the full moon that wrestled through the gray clouds to illuminate his curtainless room. Wind and hail pelted against the panes, jolting him from a comatose state of bad dreams to the tickling sensation of Loser's mangy paw crammed up his nose.

Snorting and gagging, he slapped at Loser's stinky toes and instead hit himself in the eye. Yelping in pain, he managed to push the sleeping mutt from his pillow, only to sneeze violently when fuzz and who knew what else fluttered about him. It was a terrible thing for a man to wake up to—the sight of Loser's ugly mug drooling across his pillow.

Glaring at the loose-lipped grin plastered across Loser's hairy face, Cort felt real pity for himself. It was a feeling he despised. When a foul smell pervaded the room he bolted from the bed.

"That does it," he grumbled, pushing at the rank dog. "Off the bed. No more sharing my pillow. No more drool on my covers. No—"

A scraping noise interrupted his ranting. His kitchen door was opening. Cort whirled around and for the first time realized the storm hadn't wakened him.

Someone was breaking in to his house.

Loser heard the sound, too. He snapped to attention. His propeller-sized ears stood out—as much as ears that size could stand out—and a mighty war cry, such as Cort had never heard, nor wanted to hear again, erupted from his shaggy depths.

Stunned by the unlikely actions of his otherwise lethargic dog, Cort jumped out of the way when, amazingly, the dog came to life. Yowling zealously, Loser zipped from the bed, toenails sliding on the wooden floor, his legs moving in triple time as he skidded out and around the door with a roar of wild fervor.

Cort's head was swimming, his adrenaline pumping. He'd managed to make it to the door when Loser howled like a cat caught in a fan and streaked back into the room, colliding with Cort's feet and sending both of them flying.

The next thing Cort knew, he'd landed with a thud, flat on his back with Loser's worst half draped over his face, and a rear paw rammed in each of his ears.

It was closer than Cort ever wanted to be to a dog again.

Spitting hair, he shoved the trembling mop of fur off his face.

"Loser! Dog! What's come over you?" Heavy clopping

on his hardwood floors drew his attention and, looking up, he nearly screamed himself.

Samantha—or he thought it was Samantha—stood in the doorway. Her whiskered face was shrouded with fine powdered ice. Icicles hung from her ears like sparkling earrings.

It was the strangest sight he'd ever seen. Cort thought for a moment that the hairy beast was even carrying a purse!

Samantha the donkey in earrings and a purse. It was as close to a nightmare as Cort had come in a long time.

That was until she snorted, sending a spray of melting ice all over him. "Awh—now! Why'd you go and do that?" he groaned, wiping his face, and glared at the beast—and the lady's purse hanging from her neck.

Lilly couldn't believe she'd hung her purse around Samantha's neck, couldn't believe she hoped the burro would take the note stuffed inside the purse to Cort. She couldn't believe her contractions were real. But they were, and her only hope of help was a whiskered little sweetheart with an impossible mission.

It was all true.

God sure had a sense of humor.

Thank goodness Samantha had been hanging around the house. The little darling had practically knocked the door down to help Lilly. The inspiration about the purse had just come to her as she was standing in the doorway, knowing there was no way, with the pain she was in, that she could get to her truck and drive to the hospital. The purse hanging on the coatrack had been a blessing.

After she'd accomplished sending Samantha for help, Lilly had managed to make it back to the living room. She'd pulled her quilt off the couch and spread it on the floor in front of the fire. Her contractions had eased for a while, then started back hard, grabbing her with the force of a sledgehammer. After each subsided she lay there, as she was now, exhausted and panting, delirious with worry.

Poor baby! This would be the most unfortunate child on God's green earth!

What child would want a mother who hadn't the sense to prepare for emergencies? A mother forced to resort to slinging her purse over a donkey's neck and sending her to find help?

At least Samantha was smarter than Lilly, and hopefully she'd made it to Cort's. Hopefully he was on his way this very minute. Hopefully, she thought as another contraction slammed into her, she'd make it through this.

Gripping the blanket, she tried desperately to relax, to focus on a spot on the wall as the Lamaze books taught. With her eyes clamped shut she couldn't even see the blooming wall!

How was she supposed to hang on and have this poor child when she couldn't complete the first steps?

How was she supposed to have this baby alone?

Her life was a shambles, and did God care?

Hardly!

Panicking wasn't Lilly's style. She'd never been a crybaby, but with each pain building, intensifying, she couldn't help herself. She wished for something, someone, anyone to lash out at, to latch onto. She wished she could get her hands around the neck of the jerk who'd said natural childbirth was the way to go!

Transition.

The contraction eased, the worst wave subsided. She

felt a bit of relief knowing the anger mingling with her fear had a name. Transition. She'd heard about it, seen comical movies where, because of it, the nice mother-to-be turned into an evil witch making the moviegoers laugh when the recipients of her wrath were thrown into hilarious upheaval.

But this wasn't funny.

As Lilly lay on the blanket before the slowly dwindling fire, things about her life started coming into focus—sharper, clearer.

She wished someone was there to calm her fear. To share the change the pain caused in her. Someone to stand by and hold the hand she didn't feel like giving, to mop the brow she didn't feel like having mopped. Someone beside her to love her through the good and the bad. To share the pride when all was done and they held the prize.

Lilly had no one.

No flesh and bone, no one to fill this want that had always been there inside her heart.

She was so tired. Exhaustion claimed her and she closed her eyes as the contraction ended. Her mind was too numb to feel any fear, any anger. She could only acknowledge her situation with a dull sense of wonder. Had the grannies passed through this same valley of doubt? Had they ever wished for things to be different, for someone to stand by them?

Were men really the way they believed them to be?

Lilly had always secretly wished they were wrong. She wanted to believe in heroes.

Were there any heroes out there?

Chapter Eight

Cort stared through the windshield at the tree blocking his path. He'd made it only halfway to Lilly's house, and it had taken him nearly thirty minutes. The note in the purse had been scribbled hurriedly and simply said, "Baby coming—help."

"Some cavalry we make," he growled at Loser, who cocked his head and barked once. "I guess we walk from here on in." It was Loser who growled at that. He didn't like the idea at all and showed it by scrambling to the far side of the truck. Squinting his hairy eyes, he glowered at Cort.

"Don't look at me like that. I had to bring you." Not certain when he'd make it back home, he'd snatched up Loser and hurried to the truck.

Now, reaching for the dog again, he wasn't pleased when Loser crouched against the door to avoid being snagged and drawn into the cold. His toenails scratched the seat as he tried to cling, and had Cort not been so worried about his neighbor he might have laughed.

Instead he stretched, clasped Loser about the middle and lifted him from the stranded vehicle.

He'd just started creeping down the slippery road, wondering how he would ever be able to help Lilly, when out of the darkness came Samantha, hauling her little fat body as fast as Cort had ever seen a burro move.

And she wasn't happy to see him standing there.

Cort couldn't blame her. He'd left Samantha at his place, not taking the time to lead her back home after he found the phone lines were dead and the electricity was off. However, he hadn't counted on the storm having toppled trees over the roads. And he'd never dreamed the burro would make better progress than he would. Poor Lilly. If she needed help fast, she was in trouble.

Samantha must have come to the same conclusion, because she took one look at Cort, stuck her nose in the air and clomped past him and Loser. The dog yelped, snapped at her heel and was promptly rewarded with a bump on the snout from Samantha's leg as she stopped suddenly to study the fallen tree.

Cort headed toward the ditch just as Samantha stuck her nose down and plowed past him into the lead. Cort continued on, following her, with Loser snarling all the way.

This was the burro's territory, and the best way to help Lilly was to get there by the fastest route. If that meant tailgating a burro—a very smart burro—then he'd do it.

In the next five minutes Cort slipped and slid on the ice more times than he cared to count. The night was so thick with billowing sleet and snow flurries that he couldn't see four feet in front of him. Finally for Lilly's sake he gave in, threw his leg over Samantha's back and settled in for the rest of the trip. It wasn't a pretty sight, and he thought that if any of his buddies from the show circuit saw him riding this hairy bag of lard his reputation as a serious breeder and trainer was history.

And that was before Loser got excited and nipped Samantha on the rump.

Lilly lifted her eyelids and screamed.

Not only did it feel as if she was giving birth to Attila the Hun, ice monsters were invading her home! She must be hallucinating, she thought, from the pain or too much oxygen hitting her brain from the useless breathing exercises she'd been attempting to master for the past hour and a half.

"Lilly, don't scream. It's me, Cort. I've come to help."

Lilly stared as another contraction grabbed her. "What happened to you?" she gasped, then started he-he-he-ing and puff-puff-puffing. She felt like a Saint Bernard panting on a sizzling day without any shade. She was so tired, but had caught a slight second wind somewhere along the way of total delusion and despair.

Cort wiped his ice-encrusted face, ran a hand through his mussed hair and frowned. "Samantha happened to me. The question is what's happened to you? Don't you know better than to have this baby out here in the middle of nowhere?"

The contraction peaked and held. Exhausted, but relieved that she wasn't alone anymore, Lilly squeezed her eyes shut. She clawed at the blanket and nearly wept when Cort's steady hand wrapped around hers and held on. Lilly had never been so happy to see a man in her life.

A calm, take-charge kind of man.

The type of man who would have the grannies rolling over in their graves if they knew she'd been lying here praying for Cort Wells's intervention in the birthing of her baby. It was true—she'd been trying to practice walking by faith, and somewhere along the way it hit her that she had to trust that God was going to get her through this. That no matter what happened He was in control, that for some reason Cort was just down the road at the time when she needed him and that with God's hand guiding her, Samantha was going to accomplish the task that Lilly had sent her on.

Faith.

Lilly breathed a sigh and relaxed.

Cort didn't like what was happening. For Lilly's sake he forced himself to seem calm. Truth was, he wanted to turn tail, hop on Samantha's back and ride right on out of there.

He couldn't deliver this baby!

Sure, all he'd ever wanted was a family to call his own, but that was as far as his interest went. He couldn't deliver a baby. He had never been able to watch his own horses deliver because of the way he sometimes fainted at the sight of blood.

Babies couldn't be born without a little blood being shed.

He looked at Lilly. She was sweating in obvious deep pain, but bravely managing to maintain her composure. She was squeezing the blood out of his hand and her eyes were weak with fatigue, but she had spirit. He'd known that in his barn, the moment she first spoke to him. She was as independent as they came and now she was looking at him for help. As if he was a hero.

He swallowed his fear. This was his fault. He was the one who'd lassoed her and thrown her on the ground.

He'd probably caused the early labor. He would never forgive himself for that.

"How far apart are your contractions?" he asked, astounded at the calmness in his voice. It brought boundless gratitude to Lilly's expression, which kicked his courage up a notch.

"I'm not sure. All I know is I'm not enjoying this." Her brow furrowed and she grimaced.

"Where are the keys to your truck?" He denied the urge to smooth the wrinkle from her forehead.

"In the truck," she said through gritted teeth.

"Are you up for a ride?" he asked. When she nodded he continued. "I need to get you to the hospital." Quickly he said a prayer that God would help him get her there before the baby decided to join them. But he had a bad feeling the hospital would be too little too late. "I'll be right back." He almost ran from the house. Knowing there was no time to waste, he grabbed Loser on his way out the door.

"Sorry, buddy, but it's back to the truck." Outside the wind was howling and the ice was thicker, causing every step to be treacherous. It took some effort to make it to the barn, trying to hold an unhappy dog and not fall flat on his face at the same time. It also took a lot of concentration and prayer, especially since lately it seemed the ground was the place he always ended up. He would have put Loser down, but he didn't want wet dog all over the cab of Lilly's truck. The going was rough, and he was thankful once more when Samantha came hurtling around the barn door just as he yanked it open.

He felt sorry for the old girl. She was covered in ice, but he knew she would follow the truck as she had before, and maybe when they went to pick up his truck she would go into his barn to avoid the storm—and eat the rest of his alfalfa cubes. If she didn't follow them, then Cort would have to lead her there and padlock the stall for her own good.

"It'll all work out, Samantha. You just follow us. I promise I'll take care of her." Reaching out, he scratched between Samantha's eyes. *I'm talking to a donkey.* Shaking his head at the uncharacteristic act, he climbed into the cab, turned over the ignition and praised the Lord when the ancient truck sputtered to life.

He backed out from the protection of the barn and Loser drew close. He watched Samantha as they passed her, then turned and watched her trotting next to the rear fender. Cort maneuvered the truck close to the porch before hopping out and heading inside to get Lilly.

He wished for a cell phone. His last one had been stomped by a horse the week before when it fell out of his pocket during a training session. The town of Ranger was so far away that he hadn't had time to go all the way there and pick up a new one. But it might not have done him any good anyway. Spots in Mule Hollow were dead zones when it came to signals. Still, if he had a phone he could at least have tried to call for help.

Lilly met him at the door. She was standing in the kitchen, a coat thrown over her shoulders and a little suitcase at her feet. Her face was pale and her eyes were as big as peaches, but she had a smile plastered on her face even though he could tell by the white knuckles gripping the counter that she was hurting through and through.

"I'm ready, but we better hurry, 'cause the contractions are closer." Her face contorted with pain at that moment and she would have fallen had Cort not reached her in time.

He scooped her up in his arms, grabbed the bag, glanced at the fire that still burned in the fireplace and knew he'd have to come back later to put it out and lock things up.

"Hang in there, Lilly. We're going to get you and your baby to the hospital. I promise." He'd never meant anything as much as he meant that promise. He would get her to a safe place. As long as the Lord was willing.

When Cort opened the door of the truck and gently placed her on the seat, pain was pounding through Lilly's abdomen like a jackhammer manned by the Energizer Bunny. She was hurting so much she was about to embarrass herself by screaming when the bushy-browed dog sitting in the center of the seat caught her attention. Focusing on the curious animal, she closed off some of her discomfort and forced herself to concentrate on him. He studied her with a forlorn kind of quizzical anxiety, trembling all over. His appearance actually made Lilly smile. He was such a pathetic little creature, making her want to stop everything, scoop him into her arms and love him until he wiggled with excitement instead of fright.

Reaching out, she was about to touch him when Cort yanked open the driver's door and climbed in.

"Whew, what a night." He put the truck in gear and pressed the gas pedal in one fluid motion.

What a night is the understatement of the year! she thought, bracing her hands on the dash as the truck jerked forward. She was startled when Cort shot a hand out and grabbed her elbow.

"Are you all right? This ice is making everything trickier."

"I'm fine. Go as fast as you think you can and still get us there in one piece."

Cort was already concentrating on the road, skillfully maneuvering the truck along the gravel road. Lilly was studying him, trying not to think about how close the contractions were getting, when a new one hit her.

"Ohhh!" she gasped. The dog and Cort both swung their heads to stare at her with wide eyes. "Ohhh, ohhh, I think I need to lie down—"

"Move, Loser. Down, boy!" Cort boomed, and the poor dog hopped to the floorboard, then turned and stuck his wet nose in Lilly's face.

It registered with Lilly as she fell over in the seat that Loser was a bad name for a dog. Really bad. And her pain was really bad. *Really, really bad.*

Please, Lord, don't let my child be born here in this truck! It was a fervent prayer. She was still praying when Cort stopped. He came around to her side and quickly tugged her into his arms, then stepped out into the bitter cold.

"What are you doing?" she asked, clinging to him. Trusty, surefooted Samantha came trotting up beside him.

"I'm changing trucks. I'm sorry about this, but I've got to get us past this fallen tree. My truck is on the other side. There is no time to be careful. Thank goodness Samantha can walk in all of this."

It registered to Lilly through the pain that Samantha was leading them around a huge fallen tree. Loser was following them with a disgruntled scowl. Lilly couldn't help it—her tears turned to laughter and she started giggling.

What a sight they made. A fat, bumpy donkey, a grumpy dog and she and Cort—it struck her that she was the bumpy and he was the grumpy of the two of them…or actually right now she could be both the bumpy and grumpy.

Cort shot her a glare as her giggles grew.

"Poor guy." Lilly hiccupped through the pain and the silly laughter. "Probably wondering what you got into by moving all the way out here." She rested her head on his shoulder and clutched him tighter. "I think you're a gift from God."

Beneath her, she felt him tense.

"I don't know about that, but I'm glad I was here to help," he said gruffly. They reached his big four-door truck and he carefully placed her in the back seat. Then he and Loser climbed into the front. Samantha was watching Lilly through the window as Cort started backing the truck down the road toward town. Loser stood on his back legs eyeing her curiously. His chin rested on the back of the seat and his floppy ears bebopped with every bounce of the truck.

Cort swung the big vehicle around in his driveway and then they were heading down the road again. Lilly concentrated on Loser after she lost sight of Samantha trotting behind the truck as fast as her short legs would carry her. Keeping up with the truck this far had been a losing battle and Lilly lost her in the distance. She knew she'd be safe at Cort's place, but her heart twisted when she heard Samantha's forlorn cry at being left behind. She loved that little donkey….

Weary with both fear and pain, Lilly closed her eyes and prayed. She didn't want to have this baby on the side of the road, but she knew they'd never make it to Ranger.

"How you doing back there?"

Cort's question was tense, clipped. Lilly wanted to

cry, she wanted to scream, she wanted to say that nothing was right. That her whole life wasn't right. But she didn't. How could she tell a complete stranger something that she'd tried her entire life to keep suppressed deep inside herself? You couldn't.

Renew your mind with faith.

"Not so good, but we're hanging on." She gritted out the words between clamped teeth. She'd be positive even if it killed her. She would force the darkness away and look to the light.

God was in control.

"God's in control, Lilly." Cort echoed her thoughts, slightly scaring her that he could read her so well.

His reassurance washed over her. Like words spoken straight from God, they calmed her. She smiled a thank-you into the darkness toward God and sighed with relief that He was out there. He really was, because He'd sent her three of the most awesome guardians that anyone could ever have.

A darling donkey, a delightful dog and a dashing grinch—who wasn't such a grinch after all.

Chapter Nine

Cort concentrated on getting Lilly to the nearest help. She grew quiet in the backseat. He knew she was fighting pain like a warrior. She had guts and then some. And she was depending on him. His mind was racing as he went over his options. He could try for Ranger.

Too far.

He didn't know much about the baby business, but he knew they would never make seventy miles to Ranger, even if the roads weren't ice covered.

His best bet was Mule Hollow.

Of the few women there were in Mule Hollow, most lived at Adela's apartments. Before he'd bought the ranch he'd been surprised to discover just how few ladies resided in the little town.

With the sour view of women he'd had after his wife walked out on him, the lack of females had actually been a selling point on his choosing the town as home.

What irony. For a guy who hadn't wanted even to see a woman for a year, now he was praying for God to open up the heavens and rain them down on him.

Loser's tail slapped him on the neck and Cort glanced at the mutt. He stood with his paws on the seat back staring at Lilly, and he'd started whining and wiggling like a nervous father. He moved in closer when Lilly groaned, and his shaggy tail smacked Cort in the face like an out-of-control windshield wiper. Lilly moaned again and sucked in a sharp breath. This caused the dog to jump, yelp in Cort's ear, slap his sharp paws on Cort's shoulder and start tap-dancing. Cort could almost hear him yelling, "Do something! Anything!"

Yeah, Cort, do something!

"Lilly, breathe," he coaxed, glancing over his shoulder. In the dim light he could see her eyes wide with alarm and pain. "You know, he-he-he. I think that's the way they do it."

To his immense relief he heard her copy him. "That's it, atta girl. Keep it up. We're coming up to the cross-roads. Town is not far away. Help is there."

"Thank you…I need…to push—"

"No!" Cort's heart socked him in the chest. "No pushing. No way. Town is just a bit farther. Breathe. Breathe. Suck that air in, but whatever you do, don't push!"

Panic rose like hot lava within him and he stomped the pedal as hard as he dared in the sleet. The truck fish-tailed. He let off the gas, turned the wheel, then gassed it again when he felt the tires catch and hold on the road. "No pushing," he said again. "We're going to make it."

Lord, I cannot deliver a baby in the middle of the road! Do not do this to me. Town is just two miles away.

Someone would know what to do. Adela Ledbetter had struck him as a very wise woman. Surely she'd been around many babies being born.

She would be able to help Lilly.

Lord, whatever You do, let Adela be the one to answer that door when we get there.

Glancing over his shoulder again, Cort's heart nearly broke when he met Lilly's scared eyes. They looked so frightened. She didn't want to have her baby in a truck, either. It was bad enough knowing she was going to give birth in a house out in the middle of nowhere without any benefit of state-of-the-art medical equipment in case of emergency. The least he could do was get her to where there would be the comfort of someone who'd know what to do.

Shrugging off Loser's clinging paws, he reached over the seat and took her hand from where she clung to her stomach. It was damp and trembling, and felt fragile within his large palm. Gently he squeezed it, feeling her fingers tighten around his—in a vise grip! The little lady had some strength.

"It's going to be all right, Lilly," he said. If she needed to squeeze the feeling out of his hand in order to ease her pain, then so be it. "God's here. He's watching over you."

He glanced back at her, not daring to take his eyes off the road for too long. She was drenched in perspiration and in the grip of a contraction, but she managed a nod and a feeble smile that cut Cort to the core.

"My…grannies are…probably giving…Him…grief." The words came out between clenched teeth.

They'd reached Main Street. Letting Lilly keep his hand as pain relief, Cort turned the corner with one hand on the wheel. The tires slid, then grabbed on the ice. Loser flipped onto his back, his legs churning as he slid across the seat into the door, then tumbled head-first onto the floorboard.

"Sorry, Buddy," Cort apologized, grinning—despite his anxiousness—at the astonished look on Loser's doggy face. "Keep breathing, Lilly—he-he-he…" he added for good measure.

"The he-he-ing isn't working!"

The huge old house that seemed to be the cornerstone of the old town sprang into view through the dark night. It reminded Cort of a hotel rather than a house, and he could see how easily it had been turned into apartments.

It was the prettiest sight he'd ever seen. Relief washed over him like cold water on a sizzling day.

In the darkness his headlights illuminated the front porch as he whipped into the circle drive and skidded to a stop. Thankfully there were lights in the front window. They had electricity.

His truck lights came to rest on an old pink Cadillac sitting out front, and his frenzied mind registered that it was an odd car, one he'd seen parked in town the few times he'd come in for feed.

Who would drive such a car? he wondered for a split second before he slammed the truck into Park and wrenched his door open. "We're here. No pushing yet!"

With no time to waste, he jumped from the truck. Loser followed him to the door, as ready as Cort to exit the truck.

His whiskered eyebrows shot up when Cort slammed the door, leaving him trapped inside the cab with Lilly. She was he-he-ing and huff-huffing like the little engine that could.

Cort banged on the large carved door. After just a few

moments it flew open, but it wasn't Adela who stood in the lighted doorway. Instead it was Lacy Brown who greeted him with her wild white-blond hair, a bright orange-and-yellow T-shirt, hot-pink pajama bottoms and lime-green fuzzy slippers.

She *was not* the Florence Nightingale he'd envisioned.

"I need to push!" Lilly shrieked as Cort's strong arms swept her through the doorway and into Adela's home.

"We're almost there, babe. Where's Ms. Adela?" he asked, striding toward the room Lacy pointed out for him at the front of the house.

"She left earlier to visit her sister in New Mexico for a week and I'm house-sitting," Lacy chirped, winking at Lilly. "And now I get to help deliver the first baby in Mule Hollow in ages and ages. Wow! Lay her right here, Cort. Lilly, this is gonna be exciting. God's good, isn't He?"

Cort shot her a startled look and Lilly, despite her pain, laughed. Leave it to Lacy to look at what was happening as a blessing. Lilly wanted that kind of faith…that kind of joy. Lacy had used that same joy helping in Mule Hollow's transformation, as well as when she helped track down a band of cattle rustlers. But that was a story for another time. Lilly needed to concentrate on the baby. Her pure love of the Lord was infectious and Lilly was glad to see her. She was one more blessing that God had sent Lilly's way. Delivering a baby would be a piece of cake for Lacy. With the Lord's help. Lilly needed all His help she could get.

Lacy asked Cort to knock on the doors of the apartments and wake up all the ladies to help.

Cort hesitated, and Lilly realized she was gripping his

hand like a vise. But when she released the pressure he continued to hold her hand as if it were a delicate flower. He looked from her to Lacy. He didn't want to leave her. He made her feel so special. Dampness gathered at the corners of her eyes. He was the special one.

He was wonderful. His heart was huge. Though he'd tried for some reason to hide it, she knew the truth.

Lacy slapped him on the shoulder. The sound crackled through Lilly's thoughts and jolted her from her wistful reverie.

"Hop to it, Cort. Let's get this show on the road. I'll call the ambulance, but the baby is coming fast. I need the other women."

But he didn't move.

Only when Lacy patted him on the shoulder and assured him she would take good care of Lilly did he make a move. Running a hand over her hair, he cupped her face. "You can do this, Lilly," he encouraged her, then strode from the room.

Cort was knocking on the first door he'd come to when he heard Lilly scream. He barely registered the wild-eyed woman who answered the door. She glared at him through the crack left by the bolt chain. "Baby. B-baby's coming." He knew he was stammering, but all he could think about was getting back to Lilly. Did she need him? "Please, wake up the other women and come help Lacy deliver Lilly's baby."

"Baby?"

"Yes. Help," he added over his shoulder, already racing back through the doorway leading into the main part of the house. Behind him he could hear the sleepy woman fumble with the chain, then pad down the hall banging on doors.

Cort took the elaborately carved stairs of the old mansion three at a time. Hot water and towels. Weren't those things needed when delivering a baby? He'd reached the main floor when Lacy stuck her head around the door frame.

"Towels. They're in the bathroom." She pointed across the hall, then disappeared back into the room. In two strides he was in the bathroom yanking open doors. Bingo! He snatched a towel, then grabbed the entire stack just as he heard Lacy yell his name.

As he rushed back into the hall he registered three things: first, a mass of women stampeding down the stairs, second, Lacy rushing toward him with a huge grin plastered on her face and third, the tiny infant cradled in her arms.

The tiny, blood-covered newborn...

"Uh-oh."

Cort woke to the freezing chill of cold water splashing across his face. He coughed, sputtered, fought the rivulets filling his nostrils and then coughed some more. Wiping the water out of his eyes, he realized he was surrounded by women.

One stood above him with a grin on her face and an empty pan in her hand. She was the one who'd thrown water on him! If she'd been a man he'd have belted him a good one. He gagged again, wiped more water out of his eyes and looked around at the women hovering over him. There was a woman patting him on the cheek and another fanning cold air on his chilled face. One woman stuffed a pillow under his aching head and another one threw a blanket over him and started tucking it in around him as if it was a straitjacket.

He felt like a drowned rat. From his supine position on the floor, Cort could see through the doorway into the room where Lilly was, and he caught sight of Loser cowering under the bed, leery of the whirlwind of activity. Cort didn't blame him—he wanted to hide, too. Fighting off the blanket, he started to sit up, only to be pushed back by a set of determined hands.

"Not so fast, cowboy."

Cort shot a glare at the newspaper reporter, Molly Popp, and sat up anyway. He regretted it instantly—the rudeness and the sitting up—but he didn't let it show. The other women backed away as he pushed himself off the floor, staggered then straightened.

His world tilted again when one of the ladies opened the door wider and he spied Lilly sitting up holding her baby.

She looked exhausted, but radiantly happy. She smiled at him and held out her hand toward him.

She was beaming, sitting there holding her child.

A knot formed in Cort's stomach. An ache welled within him and it was all he could do to move toward them through the doorway. He was mesmerized.

"Cort, you scared me to death. Are you okay?" She wiggled her fingers at him when he made no move to take the hand she held out to him.

He'd held her hand all through the contractions, but now, looking at her slender fingers, he was petrified as he reached out and closed his large fingers about hers.

"I'm fine," he said, his voice gruff. He pushed aside the feelings threatening to overwhelm him. "I don't seem to be able to handle the sight of blood. How are you?" he asked, changing the subject, but genuinely interested in her well-being and that of the baby nestled in her arms. They made a perfect picture of peace.

They made his heart ache.

"Worn out but ready to fly," she was saying, and he had to concentrate on her words. But his carefully constructed fortress was cracking up around him.

"Have you ever, ever in your whole life seen anything quite so beautiful?"

"Never," he said, and knew he meant it. They were a vision, mother and child. The little boy had dark hair, and a full head of it.

His children would have had dark hair.

Shards of regret flew at him, ripping at his heart, the anguish of what he'd lost fighting to be free for all to see. He tried to swallow, but his throat was dry, as if he'd just eaten a spoonful of flour.

"Okay, ambulance is on the way," Lacy said, entering the room in a flurry of color and movement.

She slapped him on the back, then hugged him, and he turned his attention back to reality and focused on her words, not his what ifs.

"You did a great job getting her here," she said. "Though I'm certain you want us all to forget about the little fainting episode, I have to tell you it was really cute."

She stepped over to Lilly and the baby and looked at him with a huge grin. "God works in weird ways sometimes. We've been trying to get Lilly to move to town. Trying to get her away from that lonely place way off out in the middle of nowhere. But she seems to like hiding out in the country all alone. Wouldn't it have been horrible had you not moved in when you did? You, Cort Wells, are a gift from God."

He was no gift, of that he was certain. But the way he saw it, God used whoever was around when the need arose. And he didn't want to think about what could have happened to Lilly if he hadn't been there. Why would she endanger her life and her baby's by stubbornly remaining alone out in the sticks with only Samantha?

But, he reminded himself, it was none of his business. It was a hard reminder. They were tied by this event, by this great adventure…by this life changing bond, but it was still none of his business.

And why did he keep thinking it was?

"Lacy, the baby came early," Lilly said, weariness weighing her words. "I was going to go stay in Ranger, near the hospital, as soon as my doctor thought the baby was ready to come."

"Yes, I know that. But you have friends here. You could have come and stayed with me and Sherri. We would have taken care of you."

Lilly blushed and looked down at her baby. "I know," she said softly.

Cort got the feeling she understood she could count on Lacy, but didn't want to count on anyone. He knew the feeling well. He didn't ever want to count on anyone again in his life.

He needed a cup of coffee. He needed to stop wondering what made his neighbor tick. He needed to pull back, step away from all the goodwill going on around him.

"You need anything?" he asked Lilly, fighting the need to take her in his arms as he had that first night in the barn. She'd felt so right.

He pushed back the sentimental yearning. Too many things about Lilly rubbed him raw, and because of that he knew nothing had changed since that first night. He still needed a good, hard, swift kick in the head.

She smiled up at him. "No," she said, reminding Cort that he'd asked her if she needed anything. "I've got everything I need right here in my arms." She kissed the top of her baby's head. "You should go get some rest, though. Because of us, you didn't get any sleep."

The picture of him lassoing her and yanking her to the floor in his horse barn flashed through his mind's eye again. "This is my fault," he said. In the distance he could hear the sound of a siren. The sound brought the full impact of the night into reality. His stomach rolled.

"How did they get here so fast?" Cort asked.

"They're not stationed in Ranger," Lacy explained. "They use the school as their central location to the surrounding areas. That way they can get to an emergency easier. But the baby came so fast I didn't have time to call until after he was born."

"Knock, knock. Can anybody join this party?"

"Clint!" Lacy exclaimed. "I'm so glad you made it before I went with Lilly to the hospital."

Cort watched her almost fly into the arms of her fiancé.

"Looks like there's been some excitement here," he said, kissing the top of Lacy's tousled hair and reaching out a hand to Cort at the same time.

They'd met at the town celebration the night before. Cort shook his hand, glad to see a male face in a sea of females.

"Excitement is a mild word for what's been going on tonight. I thought this was a quiet little town," Cort said just as he heard the ambulance whip into the drive.

When everyone's attention turned to the ambulance Cort turned back to Lilly. He was relieved she was about to get the help she needed. "You're going to be all right now," he assured her, reaching out to touch her soft cheek. "You were amazing tonight, Lilly."

The smile she gave him was tired, but her eyes were bright when she reached up and grasped his hand. "Thank you, Cort. What would I have done without you?" She said it so softly he had to lean down to hear her.

The kiss she planted on his cheek surprised him.

It was quick and neat and innocent—and had his mind reeling and his skin tingling. He wanted to take her in his arms.

"Could I ask you one more favor?"

"Anything you want," he managed to get out above the turmoil the kiss had raised in him.

"Could you look after Samantha while I'm at the hospital? It probably won't be but for today, maybe tonight."

The emergency team entered the room in a flurry. "I'll take care of everything. Don't you worry about anything but this little boy. I'm going to get out of their way now, but you take care. Okay?" He started to reach out and touch the baby's soft cheek, but stopped himself. Looking into the sleeping face of Lilly's son, he felt a band of anguish tighten around his heart. He fought the lump forming in his throat and the burning behind his eyes.

No use. Regrets belted him in the gut. Slammed into him so hard he wrenched away, hoping his pain wasn't written on his face.

It was time to go home.

It was time to get back to reality.

He'd come to Mule Hollow to make peace with God and a future he despised letting go of. And instead he'd run headlong into a wide-screen viewing of what he'd lost. Of what he'd never have.

He glanced back before he reached the door, and it took every ounce of willpower he possessed to keep going.

There was too much sitting on that bed that he'd always wanted.

God was pushing buttons he didn't need pushed.

It hit Cort as it had for the past year that sometimes God asked too much of a man.

He chanced one more look over his shoulder and watched them load Lilly onto the stretcher, then he strode from the room and out into the freezing night.

The frigid air wrapped around him like the clamp that gripped his heart.

Sometimes it wasn't easy hanging on to God. Especially when it felt as if God had turned His back on him, trashed his life and expected him to sit up and be happy about it.

Chapter Ten

Lilly was home. At least, she thought it was her home. It had been overrun with people. Good, caring people. Loving people. Esther Mae and Norma Sue had made themselves at home when Lacy and Clint brought her and her newborn, Joshua, home from the hospital.

For two days they'd taken care of her and entertained her. They were like Ethel and Lucy. Esther Mae had flaming red hair that just a few months earlier had been piled high on her head like the…well, Lilly couldn't exactly come up with an analogy of what it had looked like, but it was really bad. Then Lacy came to town, cut it off and now Esther Mae looked like a million bucks.

Most of the time.

Like Lucy, Esther Mae was loud and sometimes said the most goofball things. Things that made Lilly laugh out loud.

Norma Sue was round, had kinky gray hair, a smile that could stretch from one end of Texas to the other, and a heart just as big.

They were in the kitchen while Lilly rocked Joshua

in the rocking chair in the corner of the living room. She paused in the lullaby she was singing and listened to them. They were such dears to come and take care of her. Her grannies would have appreciated their care of her.

"So, I was telling Hank just the other day that we needed to go down there and get to know this Cort Wells," Esther Mae said.

Lilly could see them through the doorway as they cooked supper for her. She'd insisted that she was able to do for herself but they refused to listen, said they could do it for at least one more night. Lilly let them at last.

"Roy Don said he talked to him a few days after he moved in and he thought Mr. Wells was just a loner. He said he didn't get the feeling that the man was a grouch like the rumors that some of those old geezers started down at the feed store. And that was the opinion I got at the pageant when I met him."

Esther Mae sniffed. "Those old coots at the feed store need a life. Why, the man is a saint in my book. What would Applegate and Stanley know about that? The old meddlers."

"Now, Esther Mae, there you go letting things get to you. God loves those fools, too."

"No, the Bible says God has no pleasure in fools. Believe me, I looked it up. It's just like a fool to start rumors about a poor fellow before he's had a chance to take off his hat and put his feet up in a new town."

Lilly couldn't help smiling. Esther Mae always did have a way with words. Of course, the best times were when she got her words mixed up, said one thing and meant another. Everyone still picked on her about having the stinkiest feet in Mule Hollow because she told everyone she wore Neutralizer shoes, rather than

Naturalizers, because her feet were so bad. Norma Sue said Esther Mae was the only woman she knew who could take a perfectly serious sentence, change a word or two and turn it into a hilarious situation. Lilly understood, since she, too, had her own problems with words when she got tired.

"Lilly, what do you think?"

Lilly looked up from watching Joshua drift to sleep to find both women standing in the doorway.

"About?"

"About Cort Wells." Esther Mae came into the room and sat on the sofa before the fire. "Is he as grumpy as App and Stan said?"

"Does he frown all the time and snap your head off when you ask him a question about his past?" Norma Sue came to sit in the chair beside Lilly. "I mean I met him the other night, but that was just for a few minutes. A person doesn't always show all of his cards in the first game. So I was wondering what you've seen of the man. What do you think?"

"Well, I…" How to answer such questions? She hadn't exactly been around Cort *that* much. Yes, he had saved her life. Who knew what might have happened if he hadn't had the good sense to follow Samantha through the freezing sleet to her house? He was her hero. So her thoughts of him during the delivery were fond, even confusing, deep down inside.

Yes, he'd been kind of snippy in the barn after he'd thrown her to the ground. But that could simply have been due to the shock of realizing he had just roped a pregnant woman. It was a situation that seemed to highly agitate the poor man, and why not? It was pretty careless on her part to be out on such a night.

And yes, he was bossy and he got on her every nerve when he accused her of being neglectful of her pregnant state. But from where he was standing looking in, it could very easily appear that she *was* being careless. If she admitted it to herself, maybe she had been, without really realizing it. But who else was going to take care of things around here?

Despite it all, he had a way about him. A way of making her feel safe. Of making her want to be around him more.

And she couldn't explain the need that kept plaguing her to find out what had happened in his past to account for the sorrow she saw in his eyes. The man tugged at her heart as nothing ever had, despite the fact that he made her angry at nearly every meeting. Every one prior to the night he'd rescued her and helped deliver her precious baby.

She cleared her throat and smiled at the ladies. She decided it was better if no one knew the turmoil Cort caused her. She schooled her emotions so that they didn't play across her expression.

"Honestly I can only say that in such a highly stressful situation as I placed him, Cort Wells was the man for the job. He was amazing."

"My," Esther Mae said, relaxing against the cushions of Lilly's great-great-granny's couch. "That was well said. Norma Sue, don't you think that was well said?"

Norma Sue was studying Lilly with an odd expression on her face. She looked over at Esther and they held eyes for a minute. Lilly got the distinct impression that she was missing something. Something important.

"How old a man would you say this Cort Wells is?" Norma Sue's attention was back on Lilly.

Age? Age was something Lilly hadn't thought about.

She'd been raised by a band of grandmas. Age was never a factor. You were either older or you were younger. Hmm…Cort was older than her twenty-six years…but not much. "Maybe thirtysomething."

"Cute, too?" Norma raised her eyebrows and Lilly got a twinge in her gut.

"Maybe. He has a hard edge to his looks. Like a stone wall. So *cute* isn't exactly the word I would use to describe Cort. Handsome, yes."

"Then how would you describe him, Lilly?" Esther scooted forward on the couch, her elbows on her knees, fist under her chin.

Lilly glanced down at Joshua, peaceful and blissfully content, and a sense of meaning surrounded her. This child, this darling boy was actually hers. She fought away the lump that threatened a rush of tears. God had truly blessed her. Then her thoughts turned to the man who had been sent to assure her baby's safe birth, the man who had made Joshua's contentment possible, and her heart got a weird heaviness around it. "Cort's good-looking, there's no denying it. But it's the sadness in his eyes that makes him seem angry. I do wonder about that." Had she said that out loud? He'd been so wonderful to her and to Samantha, and now she was blabbing about his personal business.

Norma Sue nodded and Esther Mae smiled. Seeing them looking at her, Lilly was overtaken by a sense of dread. What was going through their minds? *Oh, no!* No…no. *"No!"*

"No what, dear?" Esther Mae cooed.

Lilly zeroed in on Esther and caught Norma with her peripheral vision. "Do not even begin to think that there is the prospect of a romance brewing here." Lilly started rocking Joshua. "My grannies, bless their souls, were telling the truth when they said the Tipps women had no luck with men. Why, you saw what happened to me. You saw what happened one after the other to my mom and grannies. Men do not—and I repeat—men do not stick around." Lilly didn't want to think about this. She had overcome it. She was a Tipps. She had reconciled herself to a life alone. She and Joshua…the first boy in a long line of girls. The first boy who would naturally carry on the Tipps name. Why, she had even gotten back her sense of humor as her pregnancy had progressed.

This wasn't a good thing, this idea of Norma and Esther's. Yes, she still daydreamed about finding the man God had made for her…but that was all it was. A daydream. And yes, Cort Wells caused her to wonder, caused her heart to skitter and lunge, but…

"I know the two of you, and Adela and Lacy, have this thing about bringing women to Mule Hollow. And I know that all the women heading this way will eventually keep y'all busy. So you can just set your sights on them and leave me out of this matchmaking plan." She was rattling. Rambling. Fumbling. "I stuck my neck out on Joshua's dad, and that landed me flat on my face in his tracks eating his dust. Nope." She rocked harder just thinking about the humiliation, the confusion. "Nada. No way. Not on your lives."

Esther smiled. "Now, hold on to your belt loops, Lilly. Do you think that Norma and I would do anything that would upset you? We know that baby doesn't need to have you all agitated. We were simply trying to get a feel for what you thought about the man. Remember, there were a few ladies there the other night when he brought you to Adela's place. We're just trying to get your opinion. Right, Norma?"

"Right, Esther. Lilly, when you said that about the sadness in his eyes, well, *naturally* we got to thinking that maybe falling in love would put a spark in the place of the sadness. God, after all, does say that it isn't good for man to be alone. Maybe Cort needs a wife. Maybe that's why God brought him to us. You do have to admit that Mule Hollow is a bit off the beaten track."

Lilly hated it, but found herself pondering the thought.

"Yeah," Esther agreed. "If it wasn't an act of God, then what in the world would have brought the man here to Mule Hollow?"

Lilly had kind of wondered the same thing. What had led the man here? When she was in pain she had thanked God for sending him here. But other than being her hero, what had caused him to move to the remote ranch?

Cort led Ringo back to his stall, then headed toward the house. The bad weather had eased up and the sun was shining bright and clear. The unpredictability of Texas weather, especially west Texas, was a factor that Cort appreciated. As the old saying went, if you didn't like the weather you were having today all you had to do was wait a day and it would change. It made winters tolerable.

The distant rumble of a truck had him pausing in the drive. For the past four days he'd watched one truck or car after another pass by as the town of Mule Hollow embraced their newest resident. He'd wondered how Lilly and Joshua were doing. He'd even tossed around the idea of checking in on them. But they'd had plenty of visitors making sure everything was all right. They didn't need him nosing around.

Besides, there was nothing for him next door except another broken heart.

Slapping his hat on his thigh, he walked the rest of the way to the house. It wasn't neighborly not to go. But then, who said he was neighborly? He hadn't seen any Mule Hollow citizens beating down his door to welcome him to town.

And that was just the way he'd planned it. They'd leave him alone and he'd leave them alone. He was the one who'd started the talk about how mean he was when he'd chosen to be so cold to everyone.

Maybe he'd made a mistake. Maybe it wouldn't hurt for him to find friends in Mule Hollow. Maybe his self-imposed solitude was off base.

Thoughts of Lilly and her baby had been repeatedly on his mind. After he'd watched them being whisked away in the ambulance four nights ago he'd driven to her house, put out the fire in her fireplace and closed the place up until her return. Then he'd gone to find Samantha.

The little donkey was nowhere to be found and he'd spent hours searching for her in the icy weather. He'd retraced his steps and found her slowly making her way toward Mule Hollow along the road at the edge of the trees. She was cold, tired and hungry, but in pursuit of Lilly. There was a loyalty in that donkey that Cort envied. He had been forced to leave her there on the side of the road, return home and get his small horse trailer. By the time he'd returned, loaded her and taken her home, the sunlight was bright in the morning sky.

Loading the obstinate animal had been an adventure of its own. Samantha wanted Lilly, and she wasn't taking no for an answer. Cort had had to use every ounce of his experience as a horseman to get the little animal into the trailer.

She had pranced and danced away from him like a

lumpy ballerina on ice. Cort had finally resorted to talking to the old girl, cajoling her with sweet talk and promises of carrots, apples and sweet feed.

Suddenly he was hit with a wave of guilt. He hadn't come through on those promises.

He paused. He should take care of that. It wouldn't hurt for him to go check on Samantha. With Lilly caring for her son, Samantha had more than likely not gotten the attention she was used to. She could probably use a little company. He sure could. Besides, if there was one thing Cort appreciated it was a sense of loyalty. Yep, he needed to make sure that Samantha's loyalty was rewarded.

Lilly wouldn't even have to know that he was out there in her barn. He'd just quietly drive over there and not disturb mom and child. Yep, they were probably holed up inside the house nice and toasty, sitting in front of a warm fire—that is, if they had enough firewood. He might check on that, too, while he was saying hi to Samantha. They would need firewood, and all those people may not have thought to check on her supply, thinking someone else had done it. He'd noticed her large stash of wood was a pretty good way from the house. Lilly shouldn't have to be lugging firewood all that distance. She wouldn't want to leave her baby alone all that time…. That's what he'd do. He'd sneak right over there and check on things. Repay Samantha for her loyalty and make sure mother and child had everything they needed.

They didn't have to know he'd even been there.

Chapter Eleven

The air was crispy cool as Lilly walked the length of her small stables. She felt more like herself with each new morning, and when she'd seen the sun peek through her curtains at sunrise she'd known it was time to try to get some chores done.

Samantha needed new straw, and that meant shoveling out the old. Lilly was actually looking forward to a little physical activity. She'd been housebound for the past few days, and the thought of using her muscles again thrilled her. There was more than enough neglected work to get her back in shape.

There was firewood to carry up closer to the house, a fence to fix—pronto—not to mention a leaky faucet that she'd been too large to get to before. Crawling under sinks when you were heavy with child was not a good thing to attempt. She knew, because she'd tried it.

She laughed, remembering squatting, or trying to squat, then maneuvering around to try to reach up and under the sink in the small space. In the end she'd lain flat on her back, arms and legs flared, as she let a cramp ease out of her side. She almost hadn't gotten up from that little debacle.

But that was while pregnant. Normally she was handy with a hammer, a wrench and almost anything else that came her way. The grannies had taught her self-sufficiency. This little ranch had been supporting itself for the past fifty or so years.

Lilly paused in her climb up the ladder and listened to the baby monitor that sat on the work bench below her. The gentle rustle of her baby wafted to her. It was a fantastic sound.

The sound of her baby.

And the sound of her baby sleeping.

She was starting to realize that not all babies slept through the night. Joshua had odd hours. Thirty minutes here, two hours there. Never, never more than two hours at a stretch. Joshua also wanted to eat all the time. Why, she had more bottles fixed and ready just to be able to keep up. Lilly had to adjust everything accordingly.

Life was not anywhere near what it had been—not that she was griping, because she wasn't. She was simply still trying to figure things out.

Norma Sue had told her to sleep when Joshua slept in order to keep herself from getting worn out. But Lilly hadn't quite figured that out yet. There were the tons of things that needed doing, and they weren't going to get done if she was sleeping or rocking Joshua.

And since she loved rocking Joshua, she'd decided to give up the sleeping. So far she was making it okay. She didn't need an abundance of sleep anyway. Things would be fine.

The fresh smell of hay filled her nostrils as she stepped gingerly off the ladder onto the wood loft. She was hurting just a little as she walked to the stacks of square hay bales. It didn't take much to prove she'd lost a little strength in the past nine months. Instead of carrying the bale of hay, she dragged it to the opening above Samantha's stall. With her pocketknife she sliced the twine, then reached for her pitchfork with her gloved hand.

Her movements were sure and easy. She'd been taught early to care for the horses that used to roam this land before Granny Gab sold them all. That had been a sad day for the Tipps household. Especially for Lilly. At ten years old she hadn't understood why suddenly Granny Gab didn't want to raise horses. Lilly shook off the hard memory and dug the fork into the sweet-smelling hay, broke it up, then tossed it down into the rack below her.

While she'd been pregnant she'd used the hay stored below in the extra stalls. But now that she could climb, she was trying to get things back to normal. The exertion felt good.

Oh, sure, she'd pay for it tomorrow, but it was worth it.

She'd worked up a good sweat in the cold shadow of the loft by the time she'd finally tossed enough hay below into the rack.

Where was Samantha anyway? The little munchkin had trotted off a little while ago, which was unusual. Normally when Lilly was outside Samantha stuck right by her side, snooping around, seeing what was going on.

Lilly walked over to the loft door and slid it back. The cold wind whipped through the opening, stinging her cheeks and making her eyes water. Whew, it was getting colder. Again.

Glancing out across the land, she could just make out the top of Cort Wells's house. His place was only about a mile from her home. Using the dirt road it was more like two. As a kid she'd taken the road less traveled. She knew every nook and cranny between her place and Leroy's old place. She'd been welcomed there then. She wondered about now, now that it was Cort's home.

Poor man. He was probably glad to be rid of her. She hadn't heard or seen anything from him since the night of Joshua's birth. She wasn't exactly sure how she felt about that.

Lilly wondered if he thought of that night. Of the way he'd held her hand. Of the gentle words of encouragement he'd said to her. She just wondered. That was all.

He'd been her dream. Her hero.

Dragging her eyes away from Cort's home, she scanned the acres around her house looking for Samantha.

Where was that long-eared little troublemaker? Leaning out the opening, Lilly held on to the door frame so she could see around the side of the barn to the house. A-hah! There she was, trotting out to the pasture, toward the firewood.

Toward the man stacking logs in his arms.

Cort—Cort Wells was here.

Lilly pulled back into the loft and scrambled for the ladder. A warm glow surged through her and a smile burst to her lips. Cort was here.

It was a good day.

Cort stacked the last pieces of wood into his arms and started for the house. The pile was too high, almost above his head, but he wanted to finish quickly. He'd stopped the truck at the edge of Lilly's drive and left it there, not wanting to disturb Lilly and her baby.

All looked quiet at the house, so maybe mother and child were taking a nap. In the daylight Lilly's house looked as if it hadn't been changed in fifty years. The old farmhouse was whitewashed, with pale yellow shutters. There was a long porch running the length of the back of the house, with many chairs fashioned from tree branches. Colorful cushions made Cort think about sitting down and having a conversation with Lilly. Maybe watching the little boy playing nearby as he grew—

In your dreams, Wells. You came to check on Samantha and carry firewood. Remember.

Forcing the ill-gotten thoughts away, he stalked toward the house. This was his third trip, because she had indeed been low in her stash next to the house. That wouldn't do in case there was another storm and the electricity went out again. She'd need the wood to stay warm.

He had gotten halfway to the house when Samantha trotted up to him. Not a stranger anymore, she nudged him with her nose until she found the pocket that held the carrots.

"Hey, Samantha. How's it going, ole girl?" Cort would have scratched her between the ears, but his hands were full. The wood had shifted as he walked across the pasture, so he concentrated on his balancing act trying to keep the short logs from tumbling out of his arms and onto the ground.

Samantha wasn't shy. She was, however, persistent. She nudged his pocket, then started nibbling at the edge of the carrot stalks that dangled from the slash pocket of his coat.

"Back off, Samantha. Mind your manners."

He tried to twist around so she couldn't get her bulging lips on the tempting treats, but she was too fast. She swished around, grasping a green stalk, then tugged. As Cort fanned his elbow out attempting to distract her, the logs tilted. He stopped, leaned to one side, bent one knee, righted, then bent the other when the wood shifted again. Samantha had no pity. She didn't care that he was wrestling with his burden. Instead she maneuvered her mouth around until she got a good grasp of the carrot and coat at the same time. Cort glanced down. "No, Samantha!" he called again just as a ragged piece of wood toppled from the stack and whacked him on the forehead, bounced off his shoulder, then hit the ground, taking his hat with it.

He staggered, and a second log would have followed if a slender gloved hand hadn't reached over his shoulder and caught it.

"My, my, my, don't you live dangerously, Mr. Wells."

His head was throbbing, but his heart was smiling. His lips were, too, because the sound of Lilly's voice just did that to him.

He'd missed her. A fact he didn't really want to admit.

He felt the carrot finally slip from his pocket and saw the plump rump of Samantha as she passed by him, trotting away with her newfound treasure sticking from her whiskered jaws. Her singed ball of a tail swung to and fro as she made her great escape. He started to shake his head then caught himself, not wanting another block of wood to fall. He needed to concentrate on keeping the pile steady.

Lilly laughed, reached down and scooped his hat off the ground. "First rule of Samantha survival—never have your hands full if you have food in your pockets. It's a no-win situation."

Cort laughed too, watching her carefully dust off his hat, then handle it gently with her gloved fingers as though not to harm it. She must have forgotten it was beyond help since Samantha had tried to eat it days ago.

"I'm beginning to understand that about Samantha," he said. "We spent an interesting night together after you were carried away in the ambulance."

"Oh, I hope she didn't cause you too much trouble."

Cort thought about the hours spent in the cold sleet coaxing the donkey into the trailer. "It wasn't any trouble. I enjoyed getting to know the little beast. I think she's human."

Lilly's eyes sparkled in the sunlight and her curls bounced beneath her red cap as she nodded agreement. He liked her red cap. It went with her cute red nose and cheeks. And her spunky personality.

"Not think. Samantha knows she's human. She just hasn't been able to convince God to give her a girlish figure so she can convince everyone else of her true identity. Here, let me straighten these up, or carry some of them." With her free hand she reached to move the disorderly wood into place and started to take some off the top.

"I've got it," Cort said, straightening and heading toward the house again. Lilly moved to walk beside him. He noticed she was nearly skipping to keep up with his long stride, so he eased up.

She smelled of hay and—what was that…baby powder? A unique combination.

"Thanks for rescuing me," he said, grinning like a fool, liking the way her eyes twinkled in acknowledgment of the smile. Also really liking the scent of her.

"It was the least I could do. Anytime you need me, just call and I'll be there to rescue you from here to eternity. And it would never be enough to pay you back for rescuing me. What are you doing here anyway?"

They had reached the house. Cort stooped and dropped the wood to the ground. Lilly's snappy lilt tugged at him. He'd come to recognize it as uniquely hers. He'd know her voice if he was blindfolded standing in a crowd of a hundred women. She sounded as if she was smiling and couldn't help it. It was nice.

Now that his hands were free, he raked one through his hair in an attempt to get it off his throbbing forehead. His fingers grazed a raw knot forming above his left eye. "I decided it was past time for me to help my neighbor. It's supposed to get really cold again and I'd noticed when I brought Samantha home that your wood was getting low."

"Oh, Cort, you're hurt."

Lilly was staring at his forehead with wide eyes. "Here, hold your hat so I can get a better look at this."

He took the hat she shoved at him, then she yanked off her leather gloves. Letting them drop to the ground, she pushed the hair back off his forehead. Her hand was warm against his cold skin.

"It's nothing," he said, making no move to get away from her gentle touch. Her eyes shifted with concern as she studied the wound. This close he could see a slight darkness beneath her eyes, a tiredness lurking underneath the spark.

Removing her hands, she stepped away. "Follow me. I need to clean that out. You have a couple of splinters in there. And I need to check on Joshua." She tucked her hands into her coat pockets.

The memory of her cozy house topped with the thought of seeing her with her son—it was a tempting picture better left alone. "I really need to get back home—"

"Men! You need my help and you're going to get it. I'm not taking no for an answer." With that she grabbed his arm and towed him toward the back door.

"You make men sound like a dirty word," he said, offering no resistance as she opened the back door and led the way into the warm house. He knew he might regret this, but she seemed so intent on taking care of him that he couldn't say no. It had been a long time since he'd felt the gentle touch of a woman. And he liked Lilly's touch.

"You have to understand my upbringing."

Cort helped Lilly remove her coat before shrugging out of his and hanging it on the rack beside hers. In her jeans and turtleneck sweater she was a charming picture with her girl-next-door beauty.

The girl next door to him.

Chapter Twelve

"**P**lease have a seat at the table. Help yourself to some coffee if you like. It's fresh. I need to check on Joshua, and then I'll grab my tweezers and peroxide." She smiled at him before turning and heading down the hallway.

Instead of sitting, Cort stayed in the hall studying the array of pictures lining the long wall. It didn't take but a few seconds to realize there were no men in any of the photos.

In the back of the house he could hear Lilly cooing and chatting with her baby. From the things she was saying he guessed she was changing a diaper. He continued to look at one picture after another of what looked to be six or seven women in various stages of their life. There were a few of Lilly growing up, and in some of them Samantha was standing beside her. No wonder their bond was so tight. They had a past together.

"Here we are," Lilly called, stepping into the hallway.

Mother and child. Cort's throat went dry watching them move toward him.

She had Joshua in her arms. He had on a cute little blue

fuzzy thing that covered him from neck to toes. There was a blue dog appliquéd on his chest. A sharp stab of regret ripped through Cort's heart and he forced it away.

"You've got a lot of pictures here." His voice sounded gruff even to his ears as he nodded toward the wall. The only picture he was interested in was the real one standing in front of him. But that was a reality he'd never know.

Why had he come here? This was slow torture.

"Yes, I have mountains of photos and I talk to them way too much. Follow me into the kitchen and I'll talk your head off while I yank those splinters out of your forehead."

Cort laughed, and despite his trepidation followed her into the kitchen. "I'm not too certain if I should take you up on such a tempting offer. You sound as if you like inflicting pain a little too much. Did I do anything to make you mad?"

She laughed. "Aw, pour yourself a cup of coffee and sit back and relax." She winked at him over her shoulder before placing Joshua in a swinglike bassinet sitting in the corner, near enough to the heater to be warm. She was a gentle mother—clucking her tongue when he started to get fussy, then smiling when he settled down. She pushed a button and the swing started to rock.

"That's a neat contraption you've got there." Cort had been guilty of walking down rows of baby items once or twice, intrigued by the items available for bringing up babies nowadays. That was before his life had fallen apart and he realized he'd never have any use for such things. That didn't stop him from admiring cool inventions.

"It was waiting for me when we came home from the

hospital. Adela gave it to us. And you don't know how many times it has saved my life. Some nights he just won't sleep and I can put him in there and it rocks him to sleep immediately."

Cort took a cup from the rack next to the coffeepot and filled it with the rich-smelling brew. "Would you like a cup?" he asked.

"Yes, please," she said as she started to heat a bottle for Joshua.

"I'll pour it, but you'll have to fix it. I don't think I can get all the additives and stirring right."

She chuckled and removed the lid of the sugar bowl.

A few minutes later, warmed by the coffee and the heater, Cort settled back and watched Lilly prepare to work on the bump on his head.

"My grannies would have had to adjust their view of men if they'd met you."

Her words startled him as much as her first touch.

"Is that so?"

"Mmm-hmm."

She was biting her lip as she gently prodded his forehead with the point of the tweezers.

She was so close. Cort studied the way her dark lashes curled. Dark and long, they fluttered as she studied the wound intently. She had a sprinkling of freckles across her nose and a tiny scar at the corner of her right eye.

"So tell me more about these grannies," he said, needing a distraction from her. He was also curious about her unusual upbringing. "It sounds and looks, from the photos in there, like they really didn't have much use for men."

Her fingers paused and she grew very still. "Well,"

she said, looking down at him, "let's just say all of them had sour experiences with men…then decided to do without them. They never knew a hero like you. It's sad, actually. I never knew one until you, either."

She blushed, then averted her eyes and studied his forehead again. Her breath feathered down around him, engulfing him.

"Ow!" he exclaimed. Thinking about what she'd said, he'd forgotten to brace himself against the tug of the tweezers.

"Sorry," she said, holding up a splinter a quarter of an inch long. "Wow, I told you…just look at this splinter! Look at the size of that bad boy."

"Is part of my brain attached to the end of it?"

Lilly laughed. "That bad, huh? I'll warn you before I yank the next one out. It doesn't look as large."

When she finally stepped away from him with not just two but three splinters, Cort was struggling. He could fight the longings that Lilly evoked in him from a distance. But with her standing so close to him, knowing all he had to do was reach out and wrap his arms around her—it was agony. At one point her lips were mere inches from his while she tried to get a good view of the last splinter.

He'd wanted nothing more than to lean into her and kiss her.

What would she think about that? he wondered. No doubt her grannies wouldn't have liked it. He knew that for a fact. No matter how much she thought their opinion would have changed if they'd gotten to know him.

"Refill?" she asked, holding the coffeepot out to him.

"I really should be going."

"Please, please stay for a few minutes. I have to feed Joshua. Please, we could light a fire and visit awhile."

Cort needed to go. He needed to get out of there. But three pleases in a row tugged at him.

"I—I don't usually get many visitors, and like you said, we are neighbors…but I understand."

She placed the pot back on its pad. Torn by feelings he didn't want to fight with, he watched her lift Joshua from the swing, then reach for the bottle she'd warmed in the microwave.

"I could stay for a few minutes." The words surprised him and filled him with anticipation. There it was again.

Anticipation had become a common feeling that wrapped around him with every thought of Lilly.

And Joshua.

Lilly beamed. "Wonderful," she quipped, and led the way into the cozy country living room. He moved to the fireplace, focusing on getting a fire going as Lilly settled into the rocker next to the window.

Cort chuckled when a big black nose flattened against the pane next to her.

Donkeys were natural guard animals. Many people used them to protect herds of cattle, sheep or goats from predators like coyotes. Cort wondered about Samantha. She seemed to have appointed herself as Lilly and Joshua's protector. Though she was a bit small for a true protector.

"Was Samantha ever used as a guard animal?" Cort asked, moving to sit on the couch, watching Lilly cradle Joshua in her arms as he greedily sucked on the bottle of formula.

"No, she was too small. That's why Leroy got her in the first place. She was smaller than most, and the breeder he bought her from had no use for her. So Leroy brought her home to help him break his bulls."

"I can see that. The first time I saw a burro breaking

a foal I was intrigued. I've never done it personally, but I know it works with cattle or colts."

Lilly laughed, tapping her fingers on the pane, drawing Samantha's eyeball to replace her nose. "The first time I saw it, it was hilarious. Docile old Samantha was harnessed to this brawny buck of a young bull and he didn't want anything to do with learning manners. He'd head to water and Samantha would just stand there with that halter stretched as taut as could be. She'd look patiently at that bull and stand her ground. She had to drop-kick him a few times when he got overzealous. In the end he was the best-mannered bull Leroy had."

"That explains a lot about her. She's a good animal."

"Nosy, spoiled and lovable. She and I have been together through so much."

Cort couldn't help but wonder what some of those things might have been.

"What happened to your husband? I know it's none of my business, but for two people who've been thrown together so much over the past few weeks, we really don't know a whole lot about each other." And he wanted to know everything about Lilly.

For a moment she continued to study Joshua's face, as if she hadn't heard him. But he could tell she was simply trying to decide whether to tell or decline. One thing he'd learned about Lilly was she did only what she wanted to do.

"He left," she said at last, looking up at the last moment to meet his gaze straight on. She gave a brief smile. A sad smile. "It wasn't meant to be. It was just one of those things in life you wish so hard for…that when the chance comes your way, even though the odds are against you, you take a risk."

Something in her voice had him wondering if he shouldn't have started the conversation. But he couldn't put his finger on what that was exactly. What did he say when he didn't have anything positive to build someone up with?

"It really wasn't all Jeff's fault. A woman should ask the man she's marrying if he wants children. I assumed way too much going into my marriage. The biggest assumption being what kind of man I was marrying."

Cort had assumed too much going into his marriage, also.

"What about you, Cort? What brought you to Mule Hollow? And if I may be so bold, why are you not married with a houseful of kids?"

Her question slammed into him, surprised him. Stalling, he let out a soft breath. "Payback time. Okay, fair is fair," he said. What did he care? "I came to Mule Hollow after my wife left me. I'm struggling to embrace the way my life has played out."

Lilly studied him for a moment, compassion in her eyes. "That happens to the best of us. I'm having a hard time dealing with the hand I've been played, also. Of course, I've got Joshua and that makes me happier about everything. Being raised by my grannies way out here in the country with no kids my age made me into a lonely recluse. At one point I dreamed of having a houseful of children someday because of my loneliness." She smiled and shrugged one shoulder. "But that was before—oh well, that's not important. I have Joshua now. That's all that counts, that I have a son. I've been blessed."

A silence stretched between them. Cort tried to think of any blessings.

"Ramona left because I couldn't give her children."

There, he'd said it. He'd spoken the words out loud for the first time.

Her eyes registered understanding. "That must have been hard. I'm sorry."

He'd never told anyone reasons for the failure of his marriage. What had he expected Lilly to say? What would anyone say to something like that?

"Do you miss her?"

Did he? Still? "Yes, sometimes. I loved my wife. But…" Opening up to Lilly was alien territory for him. Normally a private person, he didn't tell people his business. But Lilly was different. They were neighbors trying to become friends. He cleared his throat and started over. "I loved my wife. Like you, she'd always wanted a houseful of children." What could he say—that he didn't blame her? But he did. He would have stayed with Ramona no matter what. "I can't blame her totally for leaving. But I thought she was made of stronger stuff. I thought she meant her vows when she said for better or worse."

"Her betrayal still hurts."

Cort stared out the window behind Lilly. "Yeah, it hurts. I was angry, still am. But I came to Mule Hollow to come to terms with everything. Maybe there was more to the marriage's failure, more I could've done. God and I are struggling at the moment. I'm not certain what He wants from me. I'm not real excited about my life as it stands. But I'm here biding my time. Waiting."

"Ramona wanted children. What about you?" Lilly asked.

Lilly believed in shooting straight. "Yes." Regret knotted his chest. He rubbed the back of his neck and met Lilly's eyes. She looked so tired, more so with every passing minute, but there was compassion in her gaze. "I wanted kids with all my heart." What choice would Lilly have made if she'd been in Ramona's shoes? "We have to take what God lays out there for us. He knows the future, like you said. He has the plan. And obviously children aren't in my future."

"And why not?"

"I'm not planning on marrying again, for one. For two, what do I have to offer a woman? I can't give her children."

"You could adopt. Or maybe the woman will already have children. Who knows?" The encouraging lilt was back in Lilly's voice.

It wasn't as easy as she thought it was. He needed to change the subject.

"Okay, what about you? Do you plan on challenging this luck of the Tipps women? Are you going to remarry and give Joshua a daddy?"

She bit her lip. "I just had a baby. I don't want to think about anything except Joshua right now. But…I'd have said a flat no if you'd asked me before he was born. Now, looking at him…every baby deserves a daddy." She paused, studying Joshua. "I chose a real loser last time. Maybe that's what's wrong with the Tipps women. We're terrible judges of character." She looked at him and gave a halfhearted smile. "Anyway, like I said, I've just given birth and that's all I want to think about right now. God's going to have to change my mind, if it's to be."

Cort felt better about opening up. There was a comfort in knowing that they both were trying to wait on God. To trust Him. Cort had come a long way in the few weeks he'd been at Mule Hollow. He gave much of that credit to the stubborn woman sitting across from him. She'd kept him busy. He certainly hadn't envisioned anything like what had happened to him since moving down the road from Lilly. A smile spread across his face. It felt good to smile. It was getting easier. It seemed to be becoming habit around her.

"Here." Lilly startled him, popping up from the rocker and crossing to stand before him. "Hold Joshua."

"What! No, that's okay." His protest went unheard. Lilly placed the baby in his hands, then walked away so he couldn't just give Joshua back. Despite all his attempts to avoid the infant, Cort found himself holding Joshua. What if he dropped him? He only weighed something like ten pounds. And he was staring up at him with bright eyes. Man, he was a cute little thing. Cort watched, dumbstruck, as Joshua held up a fist and jerked it around a few times.

"Hey, little buddy, don't hit yourself with that thing." The words came out before he could stop them. Joshua smiled and cooed.

Cort felt stiff and awkward, but Lilly had stepped into the kitchen and was rummaging around where he couldn't see her. Cort decided he should rock, so he rocked the baby the way he'd seen Lilly doing, but it didn't feel right. It didn't look right, either. It had looked natural when she swayed back and forth. Maybe he should move to the rocking chair. But if he tripped walking over there… He'd better stay right where he was on the couch. That way no disaster could strike. He wouldn't trip over his big feet while crossing the room.

Lilly was a good mother—at least, he'd thought so before she'd decided he was a safe bet to hold her baby. He tilted Joshua a little closer to his chest so that they were actually touching. Lilly had acted as if he wouldn't break the boy. He figured she might be right.

He was getting the hang of this.

And Joshua acted as if he liked him okay.

Looking up, he found Lilly watching him from the doorway of the kitchen with a sad little smile. When she met his gaze she blinked, then the smile bloomed.

"I think he likes you, Cort."

Chapter Thirteen

Lilly followed Cort outside. She'd finally rescued him from Joshua right after her son had fallen fast asleep snuggled up against Cort's heart.

She pushed the tugging of her own heart away and concentrated on being a good neighbor. And a friend. They'd both been through a hard time—it was a bond that made her determined to befriend him.

He'd looked so cute not knowing how to hold Joshua. His look of bewilderment had sent a jolt of joy and compassion surging through her. And it had started a small idea forming at the back of her mind. It was something she'd have to think about, that she couldn't make a mistake about. It was something she'd have to spend a lot of time in prayer about. But she had a feeling she already knew what God was going to tell her.

"He went right to sleep, didn't he?" Cort's voice broke into her thoughts.

There was wonder in his words. She smiled up at him as they walked down her driveway toward his truck. The crazy guy had parked it near the road so that he wouldn't wake them up if they'd been napping. He was so sweet.

"Yes, he did go right to sleep," she agreed. "You got really good at cradling him next to you. That is after you stopped holding him out like he was going to kick you or upchuck on you." She laughed again, remembering the scene...and the ache that it had caused in her heart.

They reached the truck, and Lilly stuck her hands into her back pockets and rolled a rock with the toe of her boot. The wind had picked up and the temperature was dropping quickly. The smell of moisture rode on the cold air, of damp earth and cedar. But it was Cort's scent, spicy and masculine, that lingered in her senses, and the sweet memory of him holding her son.

"Lilly, I'd like to help you with anything I can around here. I'll come back tomorrow and finish bringing up firewood and take care of anything else you need to have done."

"I can take care of it. There's no reason for you to take time away from your horses. Really, you've done way too much for me already."

"Lilly, we're neighbors, and we've been through a lot together. I'd like to do this for you."

Lilly's first inclination was to say no again. But they *had* been through so much together. And really, she could use a little help. She just wasn't used to asking for it. "Okay, but only if you have time."

"I've come a long way since our first meeting. I'm not the nasty old ogre anymore. I hope."

"Yes. Yes, you have come a long way. I don't even recognize you." She took a step backward, yanking a thumb in the direction of the house. "I have to go inside and check on Joshua. But I'll see you tomorrow. Neighbor."

* * *

Cort watched Lilly trek up the driveway. Her hair was bouncing loose just above her collar as she tugged her coat tighter about her. "See you later," he said softly to himself. Regret settled over him. He'd come there intending to get in and out without seeing her. Now that he'd seen her he didn't want to leave. There was such a beauty that flowed from her. There was far more to Lilly than a pretty face. She had an inner beauty that glowed. That worried him.

Watching her stride away, purpose in her steps, he realized his heart was telling him, despite his efforts to convince himself otherwise, that Lilly was more than a neighbor.

Pushing the thought into the shadows, he was getting into his truck when Lilly whirled around.

"Thank you again, Cort," she called.

Cort shut down feelings tugging at his heart. "Anytime."

Her smile broadened, then she turned on her heel and hurried toward the house. She could actually move pretty fast when she wasn't waddling. He frowned. Waddling or not, Lilly made him want things. But she was too young to be saddled with a man who could never give her a family.

Joshua was going to need siblings.

A picture of Lilly and all those children he'd envisioned her with on their first meeting popped into his head.

Scowling, he turned back toward his truck and climbed in.

Who was he kidding? This attraction had him scared to death.

* * *

Lilly sat in the booth at Sam's Diner and smiled at the chaos going on around her. The jukebox, which seemed to have a mind of its own, was blasting out the strains of its latest choice, "All I Want for Christmas Is My Two Front Teeth." It had been stuck for months on Jerry Lee Lewis burning up the piano with "Great Balls of Fire," with everyone exclaiming *Goodness gracious!* every time the jukebox played. But now even the mention of wanting two front teeth for Christmas got a bad reaction.

Norma Sue had been able to at least change out the forty-five so that Sam could get some relief from the same song playing 24/7, but then she hadn't been able to get the silly Christmas tune unstuck from the holding mechanism. It never failed that someone coming into the diner stuck a nickel in the slot just to ruffle everyone's feathers.

Today Sherri and Lacy had invited her to bring Joshua to town for a hamburger. She hadn't realized they were actually throwing her a surprise baby shower. The little country diner and pharmacy was packed.

Why, there were more frilly packages stacked on the counter than Lilly had ever seen before. Birthdays at the Tipps household had always been fun, but because there had never been an abundance of people at the gatherings, or money, the gifts had been slim, but always filled with love. From the look of things here, Joshua might not need a change of clothes for years.

Frogs seemed to be the theme. Frogs and cowboys. Joshua was going to be a frog-loving cowboy. He had shirts with frogs and sleepers with frogs. He had diapers with frogs. He had red bandannas, plaid shirts and little tiny blue jeans with cowboy hats and lassos appliquéd all over them. He even had a tiny Stetson for his little head. He was going to be a lassoing cowboy who *Fully Relied On God*. Thus the F.R.O.G. theme. Lacy had come up with the idea. Lilly loved it.

"Lilly," Lacy called as she grabbed the next package in line for Lilly to open. "We tried to invite Cort to this party, but he wasn't home when I stopped by."

Lilly looked around the room full of women and wondered why they would want to invite Cort to her baby shower. Not that she wouldn't like seeing him. She would. As promised, he'd come and brought plenty of wood up to the house for easy access for her, but he hadn't stayed to talk. Instead he'd insisted he had work to do at home. Lilly tried not to let it bother her. But it did.

She'd decided the man could just stay home, for all she cared. She didn't want him coming over just because he thought she couldn't take care of her own stuff. She could. She'd agreed to let him help only because he'd acted as if he really wanted to.

Keeping her feelings to herself, Lilly offered Lacy a bright smile. "I'm sure he has things to do. Anyway, there aren't any other guys here."

"Beggin' your pardon, but I'm here," said Sam, the owner, coming out of the back carrying a cake. Samantha had been named after Sam back when he and Leroy were best friends growing up. "I ain't decided if that's a good thing or a bad thing. Thar's a lot of you gals in here. Then again, *that's* a good thing."

Lacy set a couple of presents on the table in front of Lilly. "You're right about that, Sam. I just thought since Cort helped get Joshua delivered, he might like to come. That's all. Oh Sam, that cake looks yummy. What kind is it?"

"It's an Italian cream cake," he said, carefully placing it on the table, where a bowl of punch and cookies were already waiting.

"My favorite," Sherri crooned, scooting out of the booth and going over to get a better look. When she reached a finger out and scooped a dab of icing off the plate Sam swatted her hand.

"Not yet, young lady."

"Sam, you know how I like to eat."

"Yep, that I do. But for this you have to wait till Lilly gets them presents opened, and by the looks of it, that won't be for another hour or two."

Lilly laughed. "I'd better hurry," she said, scanning the room. Molly snapped a picture of her, startling Joshua from sleep. He started to scream, immediately triggering maternal feelings from a host of ladies.

"Oh, now," Adela cooed. Being closest to him, she beat the others and competently scooped him out of his carrier.

Adela was such an elegant woman with her stylish white hair and her lean carriage. Her incisive blue eyes lit up as she cradled Joshua.

"You are such a sweet dear," she crooned, and to Lilly's surprise Joshua stopped crying, instead opting for watching her beaming face as she talked gently to him.

"Times a-wastin', Lilly," Norma Sue said. "Better get goin' on the presents or by the looks of things we might be here tomorrow."

To make them happy Lilly ripped open the brightly colored present. "I think I need some help. My arms are getting tired." They were all grinning at her and it made her heart swell with warmth. It felt good to be out. To be in this circle of friends. "It's a good thing I live alone, or else there might not be any place to put all this wonderful stuff."

Sherri slid into the seat, grabbed a present and started tearing it open. "I bet you could squeeze a man into the house even with all of this. Oh, and I'm helping 'cause I want a piece of that cake. Tonight! I've got to wait too long for Lacy's wedding cake."

Lacy set a few more presents on the table, then tapped her hot pink fingernails on the surface. "February fourteenth can't get here soon enough for me either, Sherri. But it has nothing whatsoever to do with cake."

Lilly fought off a twinge of sadness. That wedding was going to be something. The whole town was getting excited. She was so happy for Lacy. It was good Lacy had found such a wonderful man to love—not that there weren't some other great guys in Mule Hollow, because she'd learned that there were.

Despite what her grannies had taught her.

It was late in the afternoon when they loaded her truck with all the gifts and she headed the vehicle toward home. Joshua was awake as she pulled away from the diner. Every time she looked at the transformation the town had made in the months since Lacy Brown had come to town, she was amazed. The buildings that had once been just dead, weathered wood were now bright as a box of crayons with paint. The hot pink two-story building that belonged to Lacy always made her smile, remembering the day Lacy had started rolling on the vibrant paint. Boy, it had put the men in such a dither. Especially Clint Matlock. That was the day the townsfolk believe he fell in love with Lacy. Right in the middle of fighting with her over what she was doing to the town.

"Joshua, you see that building right there?" Lilly nodded toward Heavenly Inspirations. "Well, that building can be seen from all the way back at the crossroads. One day you're going to point your little finger and ask, 'What's that, Momma?'" Lilly reached over and wiggled his toe. "You are…yes, you are—that is, unless you're color-blind."

He smiled at her as she turned and headed out of town. Well, at least she was going to call what he did a smile. Everyone said three-week-old babies didn't smile, but until she got home and found proof in his diaper that he'd been up to something else, she was going to say that little Joshua smiled at the thought of seeing a bright pink building out in the middle of nowhere.

Lilly was dreaming of sleep by the time she arrived home. It had been a long day. She was now trying to heed Norma Sue's advice and sleep as much as she could when Joshua slept. But bills had to be paid, and uploading pictures and information for the catalog didn't get done while she slept.

The sun had lingered for a few days, but ice was in the forecast again. She didn't care. She and Joshua would hole up in their house and spend time together. She would work fast, get some sleep and, who knew, she might even cook. Other people had babies and took care of things at the same time. She could, too. She wasn't a superhero or anything, but she could do this.

She'd bought a small turkey before the cold weather crept in, and hadn't felt like cooking it. She might just give it a try. Yes, get the Sunday dinner tradition started again. She needed practice, because the last time she'd attempted cooking turkey and dressing had been with Granny Bunches, and that had been years ago. Sadly, with all her grannies gone, Lilly had let all traditions falter.

Things were different now. She had Joshua to think about. She had memories to make for him. That settled, she started singing a lullaby to Joshua, just as Granny Bunches had sung to her. When she finally turned her old truck onto her dirt road, she was feeling positive that she would cook that turkey. She'd practice up for next year. If she started now, by the time Thanksgiving and Christmas came around, she'd be a pro. She might even be good enough to invite people from town.

Maybe Cort would like to come? The idea struck her as she was passing his place. Yes, dinner would be a gesture of appreciation for all he'd done for her. Maybe that would help get them back to where they'd been the day he'd held Joshua.

It still bugged her. What had happened to make him seem so distant?

Though his place sat off the road a good way, she could see the entrance of his barn. She was looking that direction when a huge black horse charged out of the barn. He was flying like the wind when he actually jumped the fence and galloped out into the pasture.

Lilly didn't have to wonder but a moment about what had happened to the big horse. Samantha trotted out of the barn and stopped beside the cedar swing, threw her head back and let out a loud *Eee-haw*.

"Oh, no! I should have known you'd be up to no good," Lilly groaned, swinging her truck into the drive and heading toward her impossible ward before she let the entire stable loose. Sometimes she wished Leroy had taken the donkey with him.

Then again, what would she do if she couldn't see Samantha? She did love the little minx.

Cort knew the moment he saw Lilly's old truck that something was amiss. It took only one guess what *Miss* that might be when he opened the door of his truck and Loser bounded off the seat and scurried off around the far corner of the barn, barking. Loser barked at only one thing. Samantha.

What had the donkey done now?

He found Lilly standing with one hand on her hip, the other wrapped around a rake, and by the look on her face, he could tell she was ready for him to jump down her throat. And he might have a few weeks earlier. Sucking in a breath, he surveyed the damage and willed his temper down. Lilly obviously thought this was her fault, and she looked so contrite and cute at the same time he wanted to take her in his arms and soothe her feelings.

He was always wanting to take her in his arms…and that wasn't going to happen. He had to get a grip. He had to get out of this trap his heart was setting for him, or he was a doomed man heading for more heartbreak.

When he spied the baby carrier sitting on the bench next to the wash bay, his heart slipped another notch into the snare. He didn't want to look at Joshua. Ever since he'd held the boy, Cort hadn't been able to think straight. He'd continued to see that sad smile on Lilly's lips. He could think of nothing other than that she wanted a houseful of children—and he could never give her what she wanted.

This attraction he felt for her didn't make sense. There was no way that he could feel, this quickly, the things his heart was trying to tell him he was feeling.

No way.

But he was drawn to the baby just as he was drawn to Lilly. And his heart ached, knowing he was no good for them, knowing they were right down the road from him, but feeling they were as far away as the moon. It had been all he could do to stay away. But he had. Now here they were, on his turf, tempting him with their wholesome lure.

Lilly stepped beside him and they quietly watched Joshua sleep for a moment. He was all bundled up, his little face barely visible. Cort's heart swelled with longing for a family of his own. The nearness of Lilly, the scent of baby powder, reminded him even more of what he didn't have.

"I like watching him sleep," he said, fighting the feelings. It wasn't bad enough that he wanted to wrap his arms around Lilly—he also wanted to reach out and touch the top of the baby's head. To see if it still felt as soft as the muzzle of a horse, as he remembered. But he didn't. Touching mother or child was going to do nothing but amplify the things he couldn't allow himself to feel. Turning away, he strode to the pile of feed that littered the floor.

"Samantha did this, didn't she?" The accusation came out harsher than he'd meant.

"I'm sorry. I saw her coming out as I was passing by."

"I guess I'm gonna have to get the whip after the ole girl." He tried to joke, to relieve the tension eating at him. It didn't work. Lilly whirled toward him, eyes blazing fire.

"You wouldn't dare! True, she's being a pest, but don't even think about hurting her. I promise this isn't like her. She has never, never been this destructive."

Her words cut him to the core. "After all we've been through, you think I'd really hurt Samantha?" At least she had the decency to look confused. "Lilly, I was just joking. I wouldn't harm Samantha. I don't know what's going on with her, but after what she did for you the night Joshua was born, I wouldn't be much of a man if I hurt her. But I'm not saying I haven't been tempted to tie her to a tree." He smiled.

"Oh," she said in a breathy expulsion of air.

He reached for the rake she still held. When she didn't let go, he raised an eyebrow at her.

"You can let go now. It looks like I came home in the nick of time."

Lilly relinquished the rake, dropping her hands to fidget with the seams of her jeans. She was tired—he could see it in her eyes and in the set of her shoulders. Not that she would admit it. That would mean she was in need of help. He was quickly recognizing that she didn't like to admit she needed anything.

"You don't have any business out here trying to clean up a mess like this. Take Joshua and go on home." His words were callous, but the need to protect her was overwhelming. The sooner she went home the better.

When she didn't make a move to leave he dared to look more closely at her. Something more was wrong. The dark circles under her eyes told the story. She was more than tired. She was worn out. Maybe the baby wasn't sleeping. He should have put his foolish feelings aside and gone back down there to help her out as he'd said he would. What kind of neighbor was he anyway? What kind of man was he?

She swallowed hard and shifted from one foot to the other.

"Samantha let one of your horses out."

Chapter Fourteen

Cort's expression changed faster than she could blink. It was exactly what she'd feared. Why couldn't he have come home an hour or so later? By then she would have located the horse, had everything cleaned up and been home resting with Joshua.

Cort swung around and spotted the empty stall. "Ringo! You know it had to be him," he growled, stalking out of the stable, his expression dark. "Let me guess—he jumped the fence."

Lilly trailed him, nearly running to keep up with him. When he got outside he halted abruptly and she promptly smacked into him.

"Sorry," she said, backing away. "I was going to go after him as soon as I cleaned everything up."

Samantha chose that moment to trot around the corner. She came to a skidding stop, slapped her big ears back against her head, lifted her upper lip, exposing her teeth, and grinned like a chimpanzee.

That was not the thing to do.

Cort snorted and walked past her, but Samantha

followed right behind him. Loser trailed after the donkey, snapping at what was left of her tail. Those two were just begging for trouble. Shaking her head, Lilly backtracked to retrieve Joshua so they could tag along, too.

She shouldn't have cleaned up Samantha's mess first. She should have gone after the expensive horse. What if something happened to it? What would she do?

Please, Lord, let Ringo be okay.

But what could happen to the horse? He was just out joy running….

He'd already jumped one fence.

Oh, no! What if he was out jumping every fence he encountered? What if they couldn't find him? It wasn't normal for a horse to just jump fences. Did Ringo do this often or had he done it because of being spooked by Samantha? Oh, this wasn't good.

"You don't think he'd jump more fences, do you?" she asked, lifting a hesitant eyebrow when Cort stopped to look back at her.

"All the barbed wire in that section hasn't been changed to pipe, and there are mares on the other side that he might try to get to. If he wants over there bad enough, then he might paw into the wire or run at it and harm himself. Ringo is pretty dense for a horse. If he got too anxious, yes, he might jump again." He disappeared into the tack room, then reappeared a few seconds later with a halter and a rope. With Samantha still trailing him, he headed for his truck.

"Wait for me," Lilly called, hurrying to catch up, struggling to lug the baby and carrier across the gravel drive.

"No! You go home," Cort snapped, and pointed a long, blunt-nailed finger at Samantha. "And take this bag of trouble with you. It's starting to look like a three-ring circus around here."

Lilly bristled. "Do not tell me what to do, Cort Wells."

Holding open the driver's door, he stopped with one foot in the truck. Loser sailed past him onto the seat, rushing back and forth from him to the passenger's door watching Lilly wrench open the rear door and lift Joshua into the truck.

"At least someone is glad to see us," she muttered, reaching for the seat belt.

Cort stomped around the truck, and Lilly whirled to meet him. Slamming her hands on her hips, she glared up at him. Too tired to care whether he wanted her along or not, she wasn't prepared for the way his nearness supercharged her pulse rate.

"Lilly, this is crazy. You need to take Joshua home and get him out of this weather. It's getting colder and he's probably hungry. If he isn't now, then he will be before we get back."

Now he was trying the bad-mother routine on her! "Wait right here and I'll get his bag."

"Lilly! Take the boy home."

He was so irritating! What was the big deal about them going along? Did he dislike her company that much? Had she imagined that day she walked him to his truck that they were becoming friends? She fought the urge to concede and go home. But he needed her. Whether he thought so or not.

"Cort, what if Ringo gets cut? What if there's blood?"

His eyes stilled, studying hers. His shoulders relaxed a bit as what she was saying sank in. Lilly could feel the tension that continued to radiate from him, but her words had hit their mark and he nodded.

"Get your diaper bag." He took a step back, allowing her room to scoot past him. When her arm touched his, her mouth went dry. Her senses were getting crazy with fatigue.

Trying not to think too much about the sensations assaulting her, she snatched the diaper bag from her truck. Butterflies churned in the pit of her stomach as she made her way back to Cort. He waited beside her door, one hand resting on the top corner as he held it open for her. His other hand was stuck in his back pocket, one booted foot slightly out front, leaving his weight on the back leg. Lilly had seen a hundred other men stand the exact same way and none of them made her pulse skip. Only Cort could do that to her. He was just a man, she told herself. But no other man had ever caused her insides to melt.

She was tired.

That's all it was.

When he reached and took her elbow, she nearly jumped into the seat from the sheer shock of his touch.

Tired. Tired. Tired. The man had touched her before. But this time she'd felt…something. She was tired.

"If I can't beat you I guess I'll have to let you join me." His words slapped her in the face.

What was she kidding herself about? Obviously he got nothing out of touching her. "I reckon that's right." It took all she had to grit the words out as she stared straight ahead. What had she been thinking?

Electricity! Phooey! She was so tired she was just flat-out nutty. And that was all there was to it!

Cort drove through the pasture, figuring Ringo had headed straight toward the west boundary, where he knew he could get into some tomfoolery. He'd done this all the other times that Samantha had let him out, and thankfully, he had yet to get hurt acting silly over a bunch of females. What worried Cort the most was the show he had coming up next week. The last thing he needed were war scars on Ringo from another stallion or barbed-wire tears on his sides or his forelegs.

He should have already taken care of the fence.

Guilt swamped him.

You shouldn't have been angry at Lilly.

"Look, Lilly, I shouldn't have gotten angry like that. At you. I'm sorry."

She was sitting rigidly in the seat beside him. Her chin was up as she scanned the pasture in the waning light. Cort's insides were trembling just being near her.

"Fine," she said with a faint nod of her head. "I'll accept your apology if you'll accept mine. I should have taken care of Samantha long ago."

"I told you I'd fix it. And I didn't."

"No matter. Samantha is my responsibility, and I should never have told you I'd let you handle my problem."

The woman had to be the most exasperating female he'd ever met. Stubborn, uncooperative—

"There's Ringo!" Lilly exclaimed, pointing out across the pasture. "Oh, my! Cort, don't look…."

Fainting wasn't macho.

Not that he'd ever worried about that too much. But it was hard on a guy's ego.

Since he'd known Lilly, it seemed that he'd spent more time on the ground than at any time in his life.

Thank goodness he hadn't fainted this time. Only because it was twilight and Ringo's coat was as dark as blood, and Lilly's warning had given him time to say a prayer. God had been faithful.

Ringo's injury turned out to be merely a deep scratch on his nose that bled profusely. Lilly might be stubborn and uncooperative, but she had a beautiful heart. Warm and caring were the two adjectives he'd left off earlier. She'd felt terrible for Ringo.

Her compassion for the horse touched him. She'd been persistent, insisting that she help care for the wound.

She'd driven him mad with her nearness. The more he was around her, the more he liked her. The more he liked her, the more certain he was she needed lots of children. She had a heart for loving.

It was evident in everything she did. Loser wasn't even the same dog he'd been a month ago. That dog followed her around as if he worshiped the ground she walked on. And if he wasn't following her around he was plopped beside the baby carrier watching Joshua.

"Yep, boy, they're pretty special," Cort said, driving back up the road to his house after following Lilly and Joshua home. He'd insisted on making sure they got home safely and into the house. Lilly was worn out. It was nearly nine by the time they'd cleaned Ringo's wound, and he wanted to do everything he could to make sure she and Joshua were protected.

He hadn't been able to keep from giving Lilly a hug before he left her at her door. It had been a long day of fighting off the need, and when it came down to it he just had to give in. She actually looked as if she needed a hug.

Her look of surprise lingered. She had been wonderful taking care of the cut, making sure Cort didn't look at the dried blood, instead sending him to tend to Joshua.

He couldn't help the hug. Anyone as dedicated as

she'd been deserved more than a hug, but he didn't have a medal, and he didn't think she'd appreciate a kiss.

Though a kiss was exactly what he'd wanted to give her, he didn't think he could survive it. So he'd hugged her, and told himself it was simply a friendly hug, that it didn't mean anything.

But he was beginning to understand that he was on sinking ground.

Because watching her in action—tending to his horse, loving his dog and mothering her son—cemented Cort's resolve that Lilly was indeed a woman who needed children. She was made to give love and tenderness.

But none of his arguments could compete with how right it felt when he held her in his arms. Nothing else had ever compared to that feeling.

Sunday morning dawned bright and sunny. Lilly had been up practically all night. Joshua wasn't sleeping worth a penny, as Granny Bunches would have said. He'd cried most of the time, even when she sat in the recliner with him. Rubbing his tummy hadn't helped. Giving him a tiny dose of oil in his water hadn't helped, either, along with a host of other remedies she knew of for his little cramped stomach. Nothing helped.

She'd paced the house with him on her shoulder and prayed for hours. Samantha had circled the house looking in every window as she made the rounds from room to room. When Joshua's cries became exceptionally loud, she would smush her nose to the window and grunt. Lilly understood the sentiment well. Joshua's little tears had ceased finally, about the time the sun rose over the hill. Lilly's tears, though, had just gotten started.

Raising a baby alone was scary.

What did she know?

She'd thought about calling Norma Sue, but felt silly not being able to take care of a normal case of baby colic. She sniffed, running a shirtsleeve across her eyes.

She'd decided she was going to be on Norma's doorstep within the next few minutes if Joshua hadn't finally found relief and gone to sleep.

Lilly laid Joshua in his bed, closed the door and went to take a shower. She could see how easy it would be to get depressed when someone had had as little shut-eye as she'd been getting. She used to wonder why God made people need sleep. There were too many things she wanted to do in a day, sleep being the least of those things. She'd learned to live on little more than five hours a night. And liked it that way.

Now she daydreamed about sleep. She was a walking zombie.

Lilly had calculated the amount of rest she'd gotten in the past four days and it had been about three, maybe four hours a day. And those had been sporadic catnaps caught between Joshua's eating, sleeping and crying. So much for the traditional dinner she'd thought about cooking.

She relaxed her head against the shower tile and let the hot water soothe her muscles. She'd promised the ladies that she would take Joshua to church for the first time today and stay afterward for dinner in the small fellowship hall at the back of the building. She was so tempted to stay home and try to get a few moments of shut-eye. He was sleeping right now. The temptation to stay home was strong.

But she'd promised. She knew the ladies would be upset if they realized what a hard time she was having and that she hadn't asked for help. And she knew she could do this.

Yes, she could do this, she told herself again an hour later. It was ten-thirty. Sunday school started at ten o'clock…so she'd missed that, but she could make it to the morning service. She had prepared a bean casserole, and carried it out to the truck, and now she was gathering up all the stuff she would need for the morning. It felt as if she was moving away for a week! Or a month, she thought as she walked outside manhandling the playpen.

Opening the tailgate, she lifted the medium-sized thingamajig—oh, her mind was losing it. She couldn't even remember something as simple as *playpen* because she was so worn out. She had become a mumbling mess with lack of sleep. She would have laughed at herself—if she hadn't been so stinking tired. She was actually being worse than Esther Mae with word flubs. And that was sad.

Slamming the tailgate shut, she went back inside, and gathered the formula bottles she'd prepared. She also grabbed the diaper bag, making certain it had baby wipes and cream and a couple of changes of clothes.

Oh, and toys.

Oh…diapers! She'd almost forgotten the diapers!

She carried her load out to the truck, then headed back inside. She couldn't believe she'd forgotten to pack diapers.

Samantha had been trotting back and forth between each trip like a mother hen. Her frayed tail was wagging and her ears were perked and white smoke blew from her nostrils in the cold morning air. She waited at the back door and patiently peeked through the screen. Lilly knew if she'd really wanted to, the little burro would have opened the door with her talented lips and followed her inside.

Thankfully Leroy had realized Samantha needed to stay outside. Using cookie power, he'd trained her to wait beside the door for her treat. Stopping in the kitchen, Lilly grabbed her special donkey treat as she made the final trip, carrying Joshua and his baby carrier outside.

The expectant burro snapped up the banana Laffy Taffy and Lilly paused to watch the fuzzy girl smack away on the sweet treasure.

Their mutual love of the yellow candy stemmed from the many times in her childhood when Lilly would share her candy with Samantha as she listened to Lilly chatter about anything and everything.

They both had saddlebags to prove their love for the chewy treat.

Lilly really had to limit her own intake of the appealing taffy because of the baby weight she was struggling to lose.

Oh yeah, the dumpy, lumpy, leftover baby fat that clung to her short, stubby thighs. But that was another story.

Being tired certainly didn't bring out her sunny disposition, she thought a few moments later, driving down the dirt road. What had happened to her? Good question. She was just too tired to figure it out. It was taking all the energy she had to keep her eyes open and her focus on the road. Finding herself would just have to wait until after church, dinner, Joshua's feeding and the chores she still had to do around the farm after she arrived back home in the late afternoon.

Lilly hoped she didn't fall asleep during the service. Her first Sunday back in church, it wouldn't do to fall asleep on the pew. She chuckled when a picture of her limp, snoring form sprawled on the back pew popped into her furry brain. Fuzzy brain…well, maybe she'd meant furry because her brain was a bit past foxy-fuzzy. Oh, man…her brain was just plain fried. Pure and simple.

Chapter Fifteen

Cort stepped up onto the porch of the country church, took his hat off and sucked in a deep cold breath. Clint Matlock had stopped by the house and invited him to church and lunch. At first Cort had told him he had things to do—which he did, but nothing was pressing. Since Ringo was still healing, he had no competitions pending. He had time on his hands and he should use that time to get back to attending church each week.

Besides, Cort liked Clint. They were around the same age, give or take a few years, and they had hit it off standing in the yard, each of them with a boot propped up on the rear bumper, their arms resting on the tailgate. Clint had apologized for not coming out sooner to invite him, but explained that he'd been in court for a couple of weeks, helping prosecute some rustlers who had stolen from him a few months back. The case had taken a long time to come to trial because the same rustlers were charged in other cases, as well, and Clint had been tangled up pretty heavily in all of the messy proceedings.

Impressed by Clint's sincere invitation, Cort had

promised to visit the church. It had been a while since he'd set foot inside a church building, and he had to admit he was nervous. But he was also determined to get his walk with the Lord back on a strong path.

Hesitating outside the door, he scanned the long narrow parking lot. Lilly's truck, parked at the back near a small outer building, caught his attention. It took him a second to realize that Lilly was still in the truck, or at least he thought it was her. The door was open and she was on her knees in the seat with her back to the door. From where he was standing it looked as if she was pulling on something with every ounce of strength she had. Setting his Stetson back on his head, he headed in her direction. He'd wondered if she went to this church, but he hadn't expected that she'd be the first person he encountered. His conscience pricked him about their last meeting. He'd been avoiding her again. He wasn't proud of it, but he was flat-out running scared.

She was in the seat. Since she was scrunched up, her dress flowed from beneath her coat over her hips and hung over her shoes. The hem jiggled every time she tugged at the seat belt that restrained the baby carrier.

"Click-in, click-out…yeah, right," she was grumbling as he placed a hand on the door frame. He held back a chuckle when she expelled an exasperated breath, then tugged again. "Come on!"

"My, my, are we in a bad mood?"

She screamed, spinning around so fast she bumped her head on the rearview mirror. Her expression was comical infuriation. "Oh, it's you! You scared me."

"Are you okay?"

Slumping in the seat, she gently rubbed her temple.

"When my heart stops banging against my ribs I'll let you know. You sure know how to snare a girl."

Cort filtered what she'd said. "Excuse me?"

"I mean scare a girl. Satan is trying mighty hard to make me turn this truck around and head home. But," she said, smiling and holding up her hand in a stop motion, "I'm not buying it. I've worked too hard just to get to the parking lot. I'm not turning back now when I have the church in my sights. Do you know how much stuff you have to pack just for a trip to town when you have a baby? I'm telling you, after all the trouble it took to get here...before I'd hang 'em up and head home, I'd sit in this parking lot just to snow—show the old man that I'm not letting him get me down."

Cort smiled. "I bet you would. Can I try and free Joshua's carrier for you?"

Lilly's smile broadened, lighting her eyes with warmth. "Joshua and I would greatly appreciate that. I don't know if you've noticed, but I'm trapped, too. I caught my skirt in the...the thingamajig." She waved her hand at the seat-belt clasp. "The clasp. I'm a little tired. As you can tell."

Cort took his Bible from under his arm and set it on the truck's hood. He knew he was treading on thin ice, liking the light in her eyes, but today he was going to try again to just be a neighbor and a friend.

He leaned across Lilly, pressed the buckle release hard and pulled. Nothing happened. The soft smell of something sweet wrapped around him and it was all he could do not to turn toward Lilly and breathe deeply. "You ever had trouble with this before?"

He'd thought about her every day. Every hour.

"No, I don't know what I did. I was in a hurry trying

to goad, I mean, load all the things I would need for Joshua during church and I don't know…somehow I caught my skirt and jammed everything."

He turned his head and looked into her eyes. They were mere inches apart. He could just lean in and kiss her. She took his breath away.

Stop it, Cort.

He fumbled with the clasp and pushed the thought from his mind. He concentrated, pressed hard and yanked. The clasp relaxed, freeing the carrier. And him. "There it goes. You're good to go now. I think it just jammed when you pushed it in, and you needed a little more muscle than you have to release it." He stepped back and held a hand out to her as she slipped off the seat.

"I'll carry him," he said when she turned to reach for Joshua. She nodded and moved out of his way while he lifted the carrier out of the truck, watching not to bump it on the sides of the door. He didn't want to disturb Joshua's contentment.

"Thank you. If you'll hold him for a sec, I'll grab the rest of his stuff." She stretched into the cab and pulled out a huge yellow striped bag with a big green frog sitting at the bottom corner. As she slung it over her shoulder, it looked bigger than she was. "There, all set," she said, holding out her hands for the carrier.

Cort shook his head. "I told you I'll carry Joshua. This thing is bigger than you."

She chuckled. "I have muscles from carrying Samantha's feed."

They'd started walking toward the church and Lilly held up her arm to show her pea-sized muscle hidden beneath her coat. Cort grinned, then stepped up onto the porch and paused outside the door. He could hear music inside. They were late, but he needed to say something first.

"Lilly, I'm sorry I didn't take care of all those chores for you. I told you I'd carry her feed. From now on there's no need for you to carry anything that heavy. I don't mind helping you, and I'm sorry I haven't come by more often. I keep telling you that and I haven't done it yet. But starting now, things are going to change. I'm coming down this afternoon to help you."

"Thank you very much for your offer, Cort. But I can manage."

"Anybody ever tell you it's okay to need help every once in a while?"

"Cort, you moved here and immediately started being harassed by my donkey, then you had to put up with me having my baby, and then my donkey harassed you some more. The last thing you need is for me to keep calling you to my rescue."

He cut in on Lilly's runaway explanation. "Lilly, I didn't mind my part in the baby delivery. I keep telling you, and you don't seem to understand I was privileged to be able to help you in that situation. I'd hate to think what would have happened if I hadn't been there. Again, blowing up at you the other day wasn't right, especially since you were coming to my rescue with Ringo. Even after I was rude—"

"No," she interrupted.

How was he going to get through to her?

"I thought after the other night we were past all of this."

"Past what?"

"I thought we were friends." Friends? Was that what they were? Had they finally made it to friends? "But I guess not."

The door to the sanctuary opened, halting all conversation as a prune-faced older man stared at them with condemning eyes. Only then did Cort realize that the music had stopped and the entire congregation had turned to see what the ruckus was all about.

"Oops," Lilly quipped.

Yep, that about said it all. Cort wanted to crawl into the shrubbery and disappear. His first visit to the church and he'd disturbed the entire proceedings.

"Well, don't stand there gawkin'. Come on in."

Cort couldn't help a double take at the *happy* greeter as he motioned them inside. Sure, Cort couldn't blame the man for his sour appearance, but *really*...the man looked as if he bit lemons in two for a living. And he was the greeter. Somebody needed to do a rethink on that one.

"Sorry, Mr. Thornton," Lilly whispered, stepping inside and patting the man on the coat sleeve.

Carrying Joshua, Cort followed her inside. Lilly started down the aisle looking for a vacant pew and he followed, more than likely looking a little sour himself.

"Glad you two could join us." The booming voice drew Cort's attention to the jovial man standing in the pulpit. "Lilly, while you three get settled why don't you go ahead and introduce your guest to those who may not yet have had the opportunity to meet him?"

Lilly screeched to a halt. "Oh, hi, everyone." She gave a little wave and ducked her head slightly. "This is Cort Wells. He recently bought Leroy's place."

Cort looked around the room, relieved to see smiling faces. Many he remembered from the dinner theater. He nodded his head. If he hadn't been holding Joshua he might have turned and walked out. If there was one thing he wasn't used to it was being the center of attention. And this would qualify hands down. Lilly didn't act as if she liked it too much, either. She'd said she was a loner. Maybe he should stay by her side. Give her a little support.

"We didn't mean to disturb the services," he said.

"Nonsense," the pastor said. "We're happy you wanted to join us this morning. We are especially privileged to have the man who watches over Lilly and Joshua in our midst. Everyone stand and greet Cort and Lilly as we sing 'When We All Get to Heaven.' Oh, and don't forget to say hello to Joshua."

Lilly's eyes were twinkling when she looked up at him. "Smile, Cort, and say hello," she said with a wink just as they were engulfed.

Cowboys came from everywhere, and a few women. Cort was swarmed by hugs and handshakes, a few rowdy slaps on the back and congratulations.

In the midst of it all Clint Matlock stuck his hand out. "Glad you made it, Cort. Lilly, too. And the baby. I hope y'all are planning on staying for lunch."

"Thanks, I thought I would. I—I'm glad to be here," Cort stammered as the full force of Clint's welcome hit him. Everyone moved back to their seats, and Cort slid in next to Lilly. Joshua was on her other side and didn't give him a buffer.

Did everyone here think he and Lilly were a couple? Clint thought so. He'd said *y'all,* as in the three of you. Reaching up, Cort inserted two fingers between his throat and his shirt and tie to loosen it. He didn't need Mule Hollow to put them together. A couple of friends, yes. He was having a hard enough time keeping his mind from wishing Lilly and Joshua could be his. The last thing he needed was an entire town, already caught up in matchmaking fever, to put their sights on them.

His resolve to do the right thing might not hold up under too strong an assault. Lilly was hard enough to resist on her own. Throw in mother nature and crazy Samantha's antics and he was sinking fast.

The last thing he needed was Mule Hollow getting in on the act.

Chapter Sixteen

Lilly found a spot near the back of the room and waited for Cort to bring in the playpen. Lacy was holding Joshua, swinging him in her arms from side to side as if she was doing the twist.

"So, how's the romance going?"

Leave it to Lacy to cut to the chase. Lilly met Lacy's electric blue eyes—eyes zinging with mirth.

Honestly, Lilly didn't know how to answer the question. How was the romance going? Did they have one brewing? Did she want one to brew? She tore her gaze from Lacy's and watched Cort moving toward them, plowing through the group like a freight train barreling down the track. Oh, he was something. He could send her pulse racing like...well, like that freight train he resembled at the moment. He could also infuriate her. But he could melt her with a smile. As for romance...he didn't know she existed. She was simply the neighbor down the road he thought needed a helping hand. "There's no—"

Lacy cut her off, handing over Joshua. "Nope. Don't even deny it. Take the baby and enjoy some time with the man. You can try to deny it all day long, Lilly, but God has a plan. And I'm here to tell you that it's walking straight toward you carrying your baby's playpen. I think the luck of the Tipps ladies has turned for the better."

Lilly cradled Joshua next to her heart, watching Lacy stride away toward the food tables. Passing Cort, she slapped him on the back.

"Mighty nice of you to help out, Cort," she sang out, and kept on going.

"Did I miss something?" he asked, setting the playpen down beside Lilly.

"When it comes to Lacy Brown, we're all missing something. That girl has more zip and zing than anybody I know. She makes a tired gal like me feel like a worn-out dish towel." She also made a tired girl think. Or dream. Lilly pushed away the silly thoughts and swiped at her curly hair with the back of her hand.

Cort's hand touched hers as he reached to touch the stray curl dangling in her eye. Lilly swallowed and met his eyes as he gently pushed the piece to the side. His fingertips brushed her temple, then traced down the side of her face to cup her jaw. "Believe me, Lilly. You don't remotely resemble an old dish towel."

The touch of his fingertips froze Lilly's breath in her lungs, and his eyes reached into that dark corner of her heart that she'd been guarding so ferociously. What did she do now? Her sluggish mind was just playing tricks on her. Mean tricks.

As quickly as his touch appeared, it vanished. He withdrew his hand, tucking his fingertips into his jeans pocket. An unreadable expression flickered across his face. And then it was as if nothing had just passed between them.

"Thank you for the compliment. I think." She forced her voice to sound nonchalant. He couldn't know that he'd just rocked her world. Flipped it like a pancake— a pancake that wasn't ready to be flipped.

He was grinning that half smile of his that she had come to know, kind of a Dennis Quaid half grin that carved a vertical groove from his cheek to his jawline along the right side of his face. It was a look that would melt hearts.

"It was definitely a compliment. Here, sit down before you fall down." He pulled out a chair, gently grasped her arm and helped her sit while she continued to hold Joshua. Her entire being was tuned to him as he went about setting up the playpen.

Get a grip, Lilly! You're made of tougher stuff than this.

And she was. She reeled in her emotions and focused on instructing Cort on how to open and set up the playpen.

"Are you getting any sleep?" he asked when he finally finished and held out his arms for Joshua.

"What happened to the real Cort Wells, the one who was afraid to hold a baby?"

His eyes darkened and he frowned. "Good try at changing the subject. You need help. And I'm here. Now, hand him over and you rest. Me and Joshua are becoming fast buddies."

Lilly relinquished Joshua to him. "I'm very glad you're here. I didn't mean to sound like I wasn't." His expression was one of complete concentration as he carefully accepted Joshua. Once he held him, he simply stood looking at him. Lilly's eyes teared up, watching his face change from deep concern to a gentle softening. She wondered what he was thinking. What was going on behind those beautiful dark blue eyes of his?

So many times she'd thought about how he'd looked holding her son that night in her living room. It seemed so long ago.

When he shifted his gaze from Joshua, his eyes were bright. Lilly's heart skipped and held. Cort Wells, the man everyone had labeled a grinch, was truly touched while he held her Joshua. Tears…his eyes were bright with tears.

"I knew what you meant," he said quietly. "I'll just lay him down in here." He started to bend, then stopped. "Do you think I need to put a blanket down?"

It was all Lilly could do to hold back the emotions engulfing her. She was in a tidal wave being swept into deep water. She struggled to form coherent words. "Yes. Here, I have it in the bag." Grabbing the bag, she pulled out the thin frog-covered yellow blanket. Jumping to her feet, she hastily spread it on the bottom of the small pen and watched Cort gently start to deposit her child onto the soft nest.

He was bent over the crib holding Joshua inches from the blanket when he turned his head and looked up at her.

"On his stomach or his back?"

Lilly's heart rolled over and gave up the ghost. "His back, please. He'll look kind of like I did on our first meeting in your barn."

Cort chuckled, then placed Joshua onto his back, pulling the blanket over his little body. Before he straightened he gently ran his fingers over Joshua's hair.

It was all Lilly could do not to make a fool of herself by jumping up and hugging Cort.

"So do they eat all the time?"

Lilly looked about the room as folks piled their plates

full. Roy Don had a plate that looked like the leaning tower of *potbellies* as he strode by, beelining for a chair so he could dig in to the massive feast.

"Not really. They try to have a church fellowship every month. As you can tell, if they did it every week there wouldn't be a lot of room in this building, because everyone would have gained a hundred pounds!" She leaned in and whispered, wrinkling her nose, "I really don't think people eat this much at home."

Cort hoped not. Pulling himself away from the urge to lean in closer to Lilly, he tilted his chair back on two legs and surveyed the group. "It's nice. I never attended many fellowships where I used to go to church."

"This is actually only my second time."

"Really? I figured you'd be right in the middle of all this."

"Nope." She glanced around, then looked at him. "I told you I'm a loner by nature. I come to church, sing in the choir, then go home. The gals are all trying to force me to mingle."

"Are you serious?" Cort didn't see her as a complete loner. Maybe that explained her reason for continuing to live all alone out where she lived. It made him all the more curious about her past. "I remember Lacy saying something about trying to get you to participate more."

"Mmm-hmm. It's a good thing, too, because I talk to myself sometimes. And that's bad." She yawned. "I'm really afraid I might conk out before this ends."

Cort stood. "Come on, let's go get us a pile of food. That might wake you up." He held out his hand and helped her up.

She glanced over at Joshua, who was snoring away.

"Look at him. Just as content as can be now that I'm somewhere I can't catch a nap."

"It's because I held him."

Lilly looked up at him and frowned. "Yeah, right."

He laughed. "You hurt my feelings. You don't think I have a way with babies?"

"You didn't even know how to hold one until I forced Joshua on you."

"I'm a fast learner."

He placed his hand between her shoulder blades and gently propelled her ahead of him. They took their place in line behind Sam from the diner, and Cort tried not to think of how much he was enjoying spending time with Lilly. He tried not to analyze anything. Just to enjoy the day.

"How's that ornery old Samantha doing?" Sam asked. "That was some sight—the two of you flying down the street on fire."

"Sam, you know I've been riding since before I could walk. And you know I've ridden all kinds of different-tempered animals."

"I know that. But bein' how you were pregnant and all, I figured them talents of yours should be set aside for later." He looked at Cort. "Ain't it right that you can't ever know what an animal will do?"

"That's about right."

Lilly looked from one to the other, her eyes wide with rebuttal. Cort had come to know that look. On their first meeting he'd thought she was an outspoken person, but he'd learned she sometimes held back. Now there was no hiding the fact she was itching to say something. It was clearly marked across her pretty face and by the way that pert nose of hers crinkled between her eyes.

Cort had come to the realization that some of his earlier assumptions about Lilly were wrong.

She wasn't one-dimensional. She wasn't boring. And she wasn't the negligent person he'd originally believed her to be.

Lilly Tipps had layers.

"Why did you want to be alone?" Lilly lifted an eyebrow and the corners of her mouth in a half grin at Cort's expression of surprise at her bluntness. He'd asked if she'd like to walk for a minute while the ladies were playing with Joshua. The cold air had helped clear the fog from her brain as they slowly circled the church grounds. She'd managed earlier to corral her feelings and had convinced herself that, being as tired as she was, she was simply overwrought emotionally and that was why her heart kept acting so weird when she looked at Cort. Now she wasn't too sure what was what, as Cort studied her for a moment. Finally he shook his head and his blue eyes softened, causing her heart to dip.

"Anyone ever tell you that you're pushy?" he asked.

She laughed, and a zing of energy rippled through her tired body. "Sorry, you have to remember that I was raised by a herd of grandmothers. To say that they were blunt would be an understatement. I have to hold myself back sometimes, because it rubbed off a bit too much on me. Believe me, though, I'm mild in comparison."

"I'd have hated to be a man around all that. How many grandmothers raised you?" Cort picked up a stick and pushed at a fallen leaf. Lilly watched, thinking about the granddads she'd never known. It always brought on a sense of loss. Pushing it from her mind, she smoothed the skirt of her dress and looked out across the church lawn.

"Up until I was twelve I lived with three grandmothers," she said, smiling at the memory of her crazy life. "Then Great-Granny Shu-Shu died at the ripe old age of one hundred. Granny Gab died six years later—she was eighty-one. Then Granny Bunches—who was really my great-aunt, but I always called her Granny—died three years ago. She was ninety." She sighed. "They would have been shocked and in love with Joshua."

She felt Cort's eyes on her and glanced over at him. She saw compassion in his expression.

"I'm sorry for your loss," he said, his tone subdued. "But that must have been a great thing knowing that many people who loved you."

"It was so wonderful. And *never* boring. My grandmothers were characters."

"What about your grandfathers? You said your grandmothers had no need for men." He quirked an eyebrow.

She quirked one right back at him. "Hey, you said *I* was pushy."

He gave a waggish grin and held up his hands. "I can ask questions, too."

Lilly laughed. "Okay, for the guy who delivered my baby I guess I can tell you my family history. No, there are no grandfathers. They came, they left."

"All that bluntness run them off?"

Lilly knew he was joking, but she had always wondered if that was indeed what had happened. "Maybe."

"All of them? Every last one?" Cort's eyebrows drew together in disbelief. It was a common expression when the luck of the Tipps women was discussed.

"Granny Shu-Shu's husband left for war three years after they were married, and *chose* not to come home. He chose to abandon Granny Shu-Shu and his baby daughters, Gabriella and Beatrice. Granny Gab, my mother's mother—her husband left when he found out she was pregnant. Seems I'm not the only one who forgot to ask about children. They were married five months, and that totally ruined Granny Gab on men. My mother was raised to distrust all men and have no use of them. When my mom died, well, that was it for Granny Gab. She hated men all my life. Granny Bunches—that was Beatrice—never married. She said she trusted that there was a good man out there for her. She just couldn't distress Gabby anymore by chancing to look."

"How about your marriage?"

Lilly plunked her fist on her hip. "You don't give up, do you?"

He shrugged. "I'm a curious guy. I want to know about my friend."

Lilly started walking again and Cort fell into step beside her. "Like I said, mine lasted just over a month. But it wasn't totally due to my mouth. I think I told you that like Granny Gab I didn't discuss children with my husband. I didn't find out until I told him I was pregnant that he didn't want any." She blinked and looked away from Cort. She didn't want him to see any weakness in her eyes. She'd shed her last tear over Jeff Turner. He was a no-good loser. Exactly the kind of man she'd been warned about all her life. "I think he was just looking for a way to get out of something he'd realized he didn't want. It had only been a month, but he wasn't around much."

A few minutes passed and Cort hadn't said any platitudes. When she looked back at him, he was watching her. He stopped in the middle of the road and turned toward her.

"He was a fool," he said, meeting her eyes dead-on.

Lilly's heart picked up its pace. "I think so. I'd take Joshua over his daddy any day. Truth be told, it took me a few months to move on, but I'm fine now." And she was. "Jeff's the loser in all of this. I'm really trying to trust God and move forward." She'd been thinking the past few days about how she wasn't going to be like her grannies. True, she'd spouted off some granny euphemisms about how men were not good for much, but she didn't believe that. God had created her especially for someone. And unlike Granny Bunches, she hoped to find him someday.

She wasn't telling anyone that she was looking, though. The way this town had gone matchmaking crazy, she didn't want anybody getting ideas about fixing her up. When the right man came along God would be leading the way, and He wouldn't need any help in the matchmaking business. That's what had happened with Lacy and Clint. Their marriage was coming up in February and God had done a great job bringing Lacy cross-country to plow their cars into each other—and to fall in love.

God was the ultimate matchmaker. And she was going to trust Him.

Looking at Cort and feeling the way her heart was thundering, she wondered if she dared imagine he was already here. That he was the one.

Cort reached out and lifted her chin. "I know he was a fool for leaving Joshua," he said. "But I wasn't talking about the baby. He was a fool for leaving you."

The cold air wrapped around them, and Lilly didn't think she ever wanted to move away from the inviting warmth that radiated from Cort. His eyes searched her face like a caress and his touch against her skin was like a dream. No one had ever looked at her the way Cort did. She blinked back a tear and Cort stepped closer, wiping the tear from her cheek.

"Why are you crying, Lilly?"

She couldn't help it. Why was she crying? Was it because she was tired? Or was it because Cort was giving her a glimpse of what she'd been missing all this time? When he took her in his arms, she thought she would break.

"All men aren't fools." His breath was warm against her ear as he pulled Lilly deeper into his arms. "I know you've had a hard go of things, being on your own all this time But the grannies were wrong. You were meant to be loved."

Lilly lifted her face to his, her heart pounding in her chest. Could it be?

"Lilly." He set her away from him. "The right man is out there for you, and I believe God's going to send him to you, and you're going to have more little Joshuas to love."

Lilly blinked. She'd thought for a moment he... Lilly sucked in a deep chilling breath of air and wiped the last tear from her eyes. She'd almost made a fool of herself. He'd said they were friends. *Friends?* Of course, comforted friends.

She gave him a smile. It certainly wouldn't do for him to think she'd almost told him she loved him.

Where had that come from anyway? Sure, she'd had thoughts. Infatuations. Who wouldn't toward the man who'd come to her rescue? Who held her baby with tears in his eyes?

"I'm cold," she said, turning back toward the fellowship hall. "It's time to go in." Past time.

* * *

"You have a beautiful son, Lilly."

Lilly looked at Cort. They had come back inside and had made the rounds chatting with several tables of folks who had settled in for domino challenges. It hadn't taken long for them to end up back at the playpen watching a tuckered-out Joshua sleep. Norma Sue said that everyone had held him and played with him until he'd closed his little eyes and conked out on them.

Studying Cort, Lilly couldn't help but feel a surge of sadness. She'd started out the day totally worn out, wanting to hole up at her house and not go to church and dinner. But she'd had about the nicest day she could remember in ages. She now had a second wind and it was due in large part to Cort. He was a nice guy, but just a friend. Cort was not that much older than her. The most important thing was that he really liked Joshua.

She'd let her thoughts go crazy outside, but now everything was fine. She tucked all the displaced bits of infatuation away and chalked them up to weary emotions. The sadness was probably due to hormones, she thought. That was it. She'd heard they could act crazy after the birth of a baby. He liked her son. And that was all that counted.

Joshua chose that moment to open his eyes and let out a wail. Lilly stood and reached for him. "Whoa, baby!" she exclaimed. "Somebody needs a new diaper. Looks like duty calls."

"I'll go get us a plate of dessert while you take care of that." Cort made a face when he got a whiff of Joshua. "Whew! Son, you have been a busy boy." Reaching over, he ran two fingers over Joshua's cheek, laughing when Joshua smiled and tried to grab the moving fingers sliding past his mouth. "Looks like he's hungry, too."

"He's always hungry." Lilly watched Cort walk off. Her crazy thoughts were churning again. He was a sweet guy. He made her want to talk, which was nice. She really hadn't had anyone to talk to in a long time, other than Samantha and Joshua. She looked around the room. Lacy, Clint and Hank were laughing at something Esther Mae had said over at the table where the two couples were hard at a game of chicken-foot dominoes. Adela and Sam were chatting with Sherri and J.P. while they all played the game at a table together. Looking farther across the room, she saw many women she'd become friends with, many people with whom she could drive into town and hold a conversation, but the thing was, she was more apt to immerse herself in her books and hide away at home.

She had been forcing herself to get out more in the past three months. And for Joshua's sake she would continue to try to let herself be more outgoing. It was true—she'd been hidden out there at the end of Morning Glory Road all her life. But having a conversation with just anyone wasn't easy for her, never had been. Until she'd met Cort Wells in the middle of his cold barn.

There hadn't been one moment that she'd had a hard time talking with him.

It hit her then that actually she looked forward to having conversations with her neighbor.

That was why her emotions were so crazy. He was her friend.

Her friend who liked her son and thought her ex-husband was a fool.

Her friend who thought she'd find love.

Just not with him.

Chapter Seventeen

After lunch Norma Sue produced a volleyball and instructed a group of guys on setting up the netting. It was a pretty exciting moment for the church to realize they were actually having a church social *and* volleyball. Even if it was forty-five degrees outside.

"Why," Esther Mae huffed, "it's almost like the old days when we had children running wild around here and Norma Sue yelling for everyone to line up so she could divide up the teams. Y'all better watch out, 'cause when she comes out of the bathroom wearing those pedal pushers that touch the rim of her boots it's gonna be an all-out war. You might not know it, but that little ball of butter used to be a volleyball-playing machine."

Lilly and Cort were almost rolling on the floor laughing with the others when Norma Sue walked out in a pair of blue capris and flat-soled roping boots! She was grinning from ear to ear when she came to a halt in front of all of them, slammed her hands onto her rounded hips and shot a dour look at Esther.

"I know you all've been laughin' about me 'cause of

something Esther Mae spouted off. That's okay, 'cause I'll meet you outside—" she jerked her head to the side toward the net "—and teach you that this old lady can still serve a volleyball up with a mean overhand."

"That's more than I can do," one of the young cowboys mumbled. "I've never played this game in my life."

"You're on my team, then." Reaching down, Norma grabbed his arm and tugged him up. "You, too, Cort Wells."

Cort frowned, and Lilly thought if he could have dug a hole and crawled into it he would have. He started shaking his head, but Norma was having none of it. She had one stunned cowboy standing beside her and it was obvious she planned on having another.

The funniest thing of all was that most of the guys were wearing jeans and boots. Many of them had changed into old blue jeans and T-shirts, but there were a few like Cort who still wore their good boots, starched jeans, long-sleeved Western dress shirts—and their belts and big buckles. They were definitely not dressed for volleyball.

Did Norma care? Not one bit.

Before it was all said and done, Lilly watched her, looking like an army sergeant, directing a failing squad trying to go AOL…no, that wasn't it.

AMUCK? Nope, that wasn't it either.

AWOL? Maybe that was it.

What were those initials they used in the military? Her declining brain couldn't come up with the correct letters, but she knew whatever they were they meant AWAY.

The guys were trying to get *away* very quickly from playing out in the cold.

But in the end Norma had them all having a great

time. Even dressed in their Sunday-go-to-meetin'
clothes, as Applegate Thornton put it.

You could bet he wasn't out there getting red faced
and stirred up.

Then again, Lilly didn't care. She was watching Cort
and trying to reestablish boundaries that she'd almost let
her heart cross. She was glad to have him as her friend.

And for now that was good enough.

"That doesn't sound right," Cort said. They were
getting ready to leave the church and head home. It had
been an unusual day.

Walking over to the window of Lilly's truck, he
listened to the engine grind as she tried to start it.

He'd helped her load everything into the ancient truck,
said a reluctant goodbye, then stepped back and waited
for her to start the cold engine. He couldn't remember
the last time he'd had so much fun. Between enjoying
being around Lilly and being goaded into behaving like
a teenager by Norma Sue, he'd relaxed and found himself
thanking the good Lord for leading him to Mule Hollow.

Of course, he wasn't allowing himself to have any
misguided feelings along the lines of pushing past a
growing friendship with his incredible neighbor. He'd
had to rein in his runaway feelings when he'd held her
in his arms. Her tears had had him crazy with feelings
of protection. But he reminded himself that enjoying a
woman's company didn't mean he was thinking about
getting married. No matter how strong the feelings of
wanting to protect and care for her were.

He couldn't help smiling as Lilly, wrinkled nose and
all, leaned her head to one side, her sparkling eyes on
him. Eyes that were far too weary.

"I'm too tired to think about this," she said with a sigh.

Cort knew it was true. For a while during the day she'd seemed to get a second wind with all the laughing and kidding that had gone on during the volleyball game. But he could tell she was worn out. The full-time care of having a new baby was showing. That was where the tears had come from when they'd taken their walk. He couldn't let himself think anything other than that. He reached for the door handle and opened the truck. "Come on. Out of the truck. I'm taking you and Joshua home."

"But what about the truck?" she protested even as he was taking her arm and helping her down from the tall seat.

"I'll come back and take care of it in the morning."

"But—"

"No buts, Lilly. It has been a long a day and nobody is going to hurt that truck tonight. The most important thing is you need some rest."

Looking up at him, she stood still for a second, then reached for Joshua. "You're right and I really need to get home. I've got a lot to take care of before the night rolls in."

Cort took her by the arms, turned her toward his truck and gave her a gentle push. "You go there, and I'll bring Joshua and the diaper bag. And I'll do your chores." He was taken by surprise when she turned around and wrapped her arms around his waist.

"Thank you," she said, giving him a quick squeeze then hurrying to his truck.

Cort couldn't move. He stood watching as she opened the door and climbed into the front seat. His heart was banging against his chest, and his senses were reeling from the soft scent of her. When she looked back at him with a quizzical expression, he realized he hadn't moved from where she'd left him stunned and silent. He'd almost crossed the line of friendship earlier when she'd started to cry. It had taken everything he had to focus on what was best for Lilly.

And it had taken a simple hug of gratitude to undo all his hard work.

It was six o'clock when they pulled into Lilly's driveway. She'd rested her head against the seat and immediately fallen asleep. She'd even slept through the bumps in the dirt road. As he brought his truck to a halt next to the tidy house, he couldn't help the feeling of longing that swept over him when he glanced at mother and child sleeping contentedly.

He hated to wake her. "Lilly," he said softly, gently touching her shoulder. Her soft curls had fallen in her face. He pushed them away from her eyes and tucked them behind her ear. "Hey, sleepyhead, it's time to wake up."

She was opening her eyes when he heard the noise. Lilly heard it, too. Her eyes widened and they both jerked their doors open at the same time.

Samantha was in trouble.

The squealing sound wasn't like the awful sound she'd made the first night of their acquaintance. It was more of a whimper. A raspy, honking whimper.

Cort rounded the corner of the barn first, halting when he saw Samantha's head rammed through a spot in the stall gate that had no room for a head the size of Samantha's. How she had accomplished the impossible, Cort would never know. Lilly gasped as she stopped beside him. Her hand came to rest on his arm. Instinctively he covered it with his hand in a comforting and calming effort. They didn't need to overexcite Samantha. Cort had seen horses break their necks in less dire situations.

"Samantha, what have you done?" Lilly said. Her voice was soothingly calm and caused Samantha to focus on her.

Cort let Lilly take a step toward Samantha. He could tell that Lilly understood calm was needed. Reaching out to the burro, Lilly placed her hand on Samantha's head and gently ran a hand down her face. Samantha blinked up at her and tried to nibble at her sleeve.

"We're going to get you out of there, sweet potato. You just need to listen to me and not get excited." Cort watched Lilly and Samantha; it was obvious they had a connection that had come from years of friendship. Cort knew horses, and he knew there was a level of trust that a rider and a horse had to have in order for them to work well together. Cort saw that trust flood into Samantha's eyes when Lilly spoke. He'd known that voice of hers was like magic the first time he'd heard it—now he knew for certain it was. Samantha closed her eyes and stood calmly as he and Lilly wiggled and twisted and pushed her big hairy head all different ways trying to free her from the metal bars.

Working close beside Lilly had Cort wishing he could stand in the barn all night with her. Of course, this wouldn't do, because they had a baby waiting patiently in the truck.

Each of them took turns checking on Joshua during the hour that they worked with Samantha. "I know if she got her head in, then there's a way to get it out." He pushed his hat back on his head and rubbed his chin while he studied the situation. Samantha watched him with steady eyes and pawed her foot. "She's never done this before?"

Lilly rubbed the burro's ear. "She's done a lot of things, but never this. She got stuck in the storeroom once when the door closed behind her *after* she broke in. She had her tail hung in the tailgate of my truck. Oh, and had her topknot of mane caught in the slats of the hay bin." Lilly tousled the wiry patch of long hair that hung down between Samantha's eyes. Samantha rolled her eyes up and looked longingly at Lilly, then spread her lips and showed her big pearly whites.

Cort chuckled. "I really do think this donkey is human. And for some reason, I think she knows exactly what she's doing."

Lilly glanced up at him. "She might. She's a con artist. Aren't you, Samantha?"

Looking down at Lilly and the smile she flashed at him, he had to corral the overriding need to draw her near.

"Alfalfa!" she exclaimed, sounding as if she'd just sneezed. Slapping him on the shoulder, she said, "We need alfalfa."

"What's on your mind?"

"Give me a second."

She trotted down to the closet door at the back of the barn, then reached up and released the latch that was almost at the top of the door. It wasn't hard to understand why it was up so high. He was going to have to raise his latches higher to keep pesky Samantha out.

A few seconds later Lilly emerged with a bucket of cubes.

Samantha's ears immediately stood at attention. She slapped her tail from side to side and eyed the bucket as Lilly came to a halt in front of her.

"I bet she can get out of there if she wants to."

Cort nodded his head. "Yup, I think you're right. At

first I didn't want to startle her, because I thought she would hurt herself. But she's smarter than any horse I've ever known."

Lilly took a cube and held it out to Samantha. She tried to take it in her mouth, but Lilly moved away. Samantha's eyeballs rolled toward Lilly, then back to the alfalfa cube, shot over to Cort then back to Lilly. She wiggled like a puppy getting a T-bone steak. Cort chuckled. The burro did love her alfalfa.

"Set that bucket down right there," Cort said. Turning away, he walked over to Lilly and took her hand. "Let's go out and see what happens."

"Exactly what I was thinking." Lilly left the bucket on the ground and let him lead the way out of the barn. Once they were out of Samantha's sight, they raced like a couple of kids to the opposite end of the barn and peeked around the corner. Samantha still had her eyes on the bucket, and as they watched she stretched her neck out so that the top of her head sank into her neck— and she slid her head right out from between the bars.

Lilly had already unlatched the gate, so Samantha just gave it a nudge with her nose, then trotted right over to bury her head in the bucket.

"Why, the little sneaky piglet," Lilly gasped.

"I wouldn't have believed it if I hadn't seen it," Cort said in a loud whisper against Lilly's ear. He'd almost missed Samantha's great escape because he'd been too busy studying Lilly's profile. He did a hasty step away from her when she turned her head toward him. It was that step back that saved him. Another second and he'd have placed a kiss on the tip of her perfectly upturned, cute-as-a-button nose. It was getting hard to stop actions that seemed natural. He decided right then and there that when he got home he was going to have a powwow with the good Lord. There were some things that a man couldn't handle on his own and it was time to hit his knees and pray for discernment.

Cort moved around Lilly's kitchen like a man with a mission. After being tricked by Samantha, Lilly had insisted on fixing Cort dinner. But he wouldn't hear of it and instead had talked her into allowing him to prepare her dinner. She had never before had a man cook for her. She stifled a yawn and hoped she would get to enjoy the masterpiece he was concocting and didn't wind up falling asleep with her face in the plate. It had been a long day, but one of the best in her life. She'd been day-dreaming about sleep ever since Joshua's birth, but right now she wanted to do nothing except sit there and enjoy watching Cort. She prayed that the yawns would go away and God would give her a second, no, make that a third wind. Maybe He would allow her to have a moment with this wonderful man. Cort's sweetness was emerging, and she was enamored with it.

"Ketchup?" the wonderful man asked. The smile he gave her was half silly as he slapped a hand towel over his shoulder then headed toward the refrigerator, his eyebrow lifted in question.

"You're getting warm," she teased. Shifting Joshua in her arms, she straightened the bottle so he could get the last of the formula into his growing little tummy.

Cort yanked the fridge door a mite too hard and one of Joshua's formula bottles flew out of the holder on the door straight at him like a fastball.

"Whoa, where'd that come from?" he said, catching it just before it hit the floor.

"I'm prepared. When Joshua wakes at night I'm bumping into walls, so I was afraid to try to mix formula with my mind—let me rephrase that—I was afraid to mix formula *without* my mind. I know I forget words when I'm tired—I don't want to think about what else I might be forgetting."

Cort found the ketchup. He chuckled, turning toward her. Lilly liked his laugh. It was low and gruff, and sent a shiver of delight coursing through her, making her want to do something really funny just to hear it again.

"I'm sure Josh thanks you." Cort dumped a good half cup of ketchup into the dish that Lilly had yet to put a name to, then cracked four eggs on the edge of the skillet, dropping them in one at a time. When he'd finished he took a wire whisk and went to town beating the mixture. She began to think it was some kind of omelet, scrambled. It looked awful, but smelled great.

She'd been thinking about her truck. It couldn't have picked a worse time to conk out on her. "Do you think my truck will be running tomorrow? Joshua has a doctor's appointment in the afternoon."

Cort brought two plates to the table with the scrambled egg mixture and toast. "What time?"

"It's not until three o'clock."

"I'll check it out first thing in the morning after I've exercised my horses. If it's just the battery and I can jump it with battery cables, then you'll be ready to go. If not, then I'll take you to the appointment and pick up the parts I'll need to fix it while you and Joshua are seeing the doctor."

"Oh, no, I couldn't ask you to do that," Lilly exclaimed. His hand on hers halted her protest.

"Lilly, you didn't ask. I offered. When are you going

to just let me help because I want to? Besides, as tired as you are, you don't need to be driving all that way alone. It's okay to have a little support."

Lilly's heart melted a little more. He could help her all he wanted.

Chapter Eighteen

Cort unhooked the battery cables from Lilly's truck. Once he'd opened the hood of the old truck, it had been obvious that aside from the fact that she probably needed a new vehicle, the battery had seen better days. He couldn't even jump-start it. He didn't know anything about Lilly's financial situation. He didn't know if she drove the old truck because she had to or because she wanted to. He didn't like the idea of her and Joshua being on the road alone in unreliable transportation.

"Loser, load up," he called out. Loser lay beneath the oak tree next to the church. Tail dragging, the lazy beast plodded over to the truck and hopped in. Cort watched with amusement.

"Perk up, boy, we're going over to Lilly's, and I *know* you want to see her." Yesterday had been a good day. No, it had been a great day. No amount of denial could change the fact that he enjoyed Lilly's company. He knew it was bad, but he'd been happy when he realized her battery was in such bad shape, and he'd get to escort her to Ranger. Lilly and Joshua. Thinking about the little boy put a smile on his face. He'd come a long way since the night Lilly had practically forced him to hold the baby. As if she'd sensed how scared he was, but understood how much he wanted to cuddle the little fella. Now he couldn't wait to have any excuse to be near Joshua and Lilly. His heart was getting involved, and it terrified him.

Basically, he was in a mess. He'd spent time in prayer and in searching his Bible that morning looking for some kind of peace about what God wanted from him. But God answered prayers in His time and Cort had come away empty-handed.

So he'd come up with a plan of his own while waiting on the Lord's plan to reveal itself. Obviously he'd been put there to watch over Lilly and Joshua, so he would. He'd help out when they needed him. He'd look out for their well-being. God had actually given him a gift. He could be like an uncle to Joshua. All he had to do was remember that anything more than friendship with Lilly would not be in the best interests of Lilly and Joshua.

Lilly had said she'd made a mistake in choosing her first husband. Sweet Lilly, sheltered by her grannies. Her ex-husband had, in Cort's mind, taken advantage of her limited experience. If Cort's purpose was to be there to help protect them, so be it. The next bozo that came to fix Lilly's roof or anything else was going to have to pass through him to get to her.

Unless Cort thought his intentions were honorable.

Then it would be in Lilly's best interests for Cort to step out of the way.

He started his truck and backed out of the drive as he glanced heavenward. God would give him the strength to do what he needed to do. He'd struggled since

Ramona left. He'd become less and less inclined to seek after God, to really rely on Him. His anger at all that had happened had put a gulf between them. Last night he'd taken a step toward reconnecting with God. He'd felt God's presence beside him and Lilly as they stood together in the churchyard. It had been God who'd enabled him to focus on being Lilly's friend.

He'd understood while looking into her sad eyes that God was with him. Because if he'd been relying on his strength alone he'd have said things to her yesterday that would only have messed up her life later on.

No matter how confused his life seemed, Cort knew and believed that God had a plan. He just had to keep treading water until he found solid ground.

Samantha was sitting on the side of the road between his and Lilly's house as Cort drove down the long, lonesome dirt road. She looked like a big dog relaxing on its haunches beneath the branches of an oak tree. A long blade of hay stuck from her mouth and she chewed it slowly, watching as Cort eased his truck up beside her.

Loser leaped through the open window and thudded to the ground at Samantha's feet like a bag of rocks.

Samantha looked down her broad nose at him sprawled out before her and continued chewing on the stalk of hay as if nothing unusual had just happened.

Cort propped his arm on the door and watched the pair. They had a connection. He wasn't sure where it would lead, but just seeing Samantha perk up Loser was a kick in the pants. As he watched, Loser rolled over, picked himself up off the ground and, lifting his head, sniffed at the hairy chin of the burro before circling her in wary discovery. When he got too close

Samantha bumped him with her nose and kept on chomping. Cort laughed. They were quite a pair.

Putting the truck in gear, he left Loser to walk the rest of the way to Lilly's. Exercise would do the lazy pooch some good. And maybe he'd learn to be civil to Samantha.

It was a nice day for a drive. The weather was cold but the sun was out. Cort liked this temperature. In the summers he had to rise before dawn so he could have his stables completely ridden before noon, just so the heat wouldn't overcome him. This was a time of year the horses loved, and he could get more out of them when they were happy. Today was a breezy, perfect day. A perfect day for a ride into town with Lilly.

Lilly was waiting when he pulled up to the house. She had on tan pants and a green shirt that brought out the gold flecks in her eyes. Her hair was loose, touching the collar of her coat, and it swayed with the breeze as she walked toward him carrying Joshua in the heavy car seat. Cort hopped from the truck to help.

"Hey, cowboy," she said as he took the carrier out of her hands. "Do you think I'm too weak to carry that?"

He smiled. She thought she was Mighty Mouse. "Nope, just don't want you carrying it while I'm around. Did you get any sleep? You look good." He was rewarded with a pretty blush.

"As a matter of fact, I did. When he woke the first time I cheated and gave him a little baby rice with his formula like Esther Mae told me to do. He loved it. He slept the rest of the night. I think the poor boy was starving. Of course, when I woke up this morning I was scared to death that something was wrong. But he was just as happy as a clam when I charged into his room."

"Well, that sounds promising."

Lilly beamed, her eyes brighter with the extra rest. "Now, I just hope the doctor doesn't get mad at me."

Cort clicked Joshua into the backseat. When he turned and closed the door Lilly was standing beside him. He had to fight the urge to hug her. She smelled so good, like fresh soap and baby powder. He opened the passenger's door and forced himself to merely hold out his hand for hers. She looked at his hand, then back at his face.

When she lifted her hand and placed it in his, their eyes met and held for the briefest moment. In that second he wished…but it could never be right, so he pressed the wish away.

"You know," she said, looking away and climbing into the cab, "your cooking for me last night was a first. And all this helping me into the truck—I wonder if any of my grannies ever had a man do this sort of thing for them?"

Cort shrugged. "My mother taught me to open doors for ladies. She would have skinned me alive if I hadn't."

A tiny smile quirked the corners of her mouth. Cort closed the door, jogged around to his side of the truck and climbed in. Lilly was an unusual woman brought up by unusual women. Her story intrigued him as much as she did. He couldn't imagine how a man could walk out on a woman carrying his child, how he could marry her and not treat her right. How he could do any of those things when that woman was Lilly was especially bizarre.

"You have everything you need?" he asked, determined more than ever to show Lilly she was special and deserved to be treated that way. Friends could do that.

"I'm wonderful. Thanks. Oh, Cort, look!" she exclaimed, pointing toward the road. Samantha was moseying up the drive with Loser trailing right behind her. They had the slow rhythm of lumbering elephants. It was pathetic.

"Loser has come to visit!" Lilly exclaimed, opening the truck door. She hopped out and jogged over to the dejected animals, giving each of them a hug.

Cort laughed, watching Loser wiggle like crazy. Why, the tangled heap of depression practically had his tongue hanging out. No, he *did* have his tongue hanging out lapping at Lilly's face, making her laugh out loud while dodging his wet kiss. When he tried to put his paws on her, Cort decided it was time he corralled his pet.

By the time he made it to her side Loser had knocked her to the ground.

"What do you feed this animal?" she squealed, pushing at the dog, laughing so hard she was making little progress at keeping the excited mutt at bay.

"Obviously not the right thing, according to his manners. Loser! No."

Reaching down, he took Lilly's hand and pulled her off the ground. Her eyes were twinkling and she didn't seem upset by the dust that clung to her. Instead she slapped her hands on her pant legs as dust rose in a plume about her.

"Loser sure knows how to mess a girl up."

He wanted to tell her that nothing could mess her up, but he couldn't say that. "He's a goofball," he said instead, then reached to pluck a piece of grass off her forehead. "Missed a piece." His fingers found their way back to the curl that dangled over her eye. She swallowed hard, looked away and took a step back.

Cort's survival instinct held him firmly to the ground she'd retreated from, and he stuffed his fingertips into the edge of his jeans pockets. "We'd better hit the road or we'll be late."

She nodded. "My grannies would be shamed by my struggles to be on time lately. But I had to say hi to Loser. He's my buddy and I haven't seen him much. Unlike Samantha, he doesn't come visiting. I smile every time I remember how nervous he was on the wild ride to town to deliver Joshua. I think he was worse than an expectant father."

Cort led the way back to the truck, remembering not only Loser but the entire night. "He was pretty bad. But at least he didn't faint."

That got him a huge grin. "Ah, don't beat yourself up about that. It was cute and terrifying at the same time. I doubt anyone had more excitement during a delivery than me. My gosh. What a night."

"Yeah, what a night."

They stood there grinning at each other, sharing a moment that connected them forever. Cort was the first to clear his throat and move back toward the truck. "I guess we better go."

"Yeah. Can't have the baby being late for his appointment."

Determined to stay focused, he loaded up and headed toward Ranger. Despite the friction bouncing between them, a shallow ease nestled about them as the miles ticked by. Cort liked the straightforward way that Lilly had of talking to him. She was funny and smart. They were about halfway to Ranger when he asked her how she supported herself. He knew the small operation she had going on at her farm wouldn't be able to do it. He was being nosy, but at this point he didn't care. His curiosity was getting the better of him.

"Besides leasing some of my land to my neighbor on the far side of me, and my pitifully small cattle operation,

I keep the books for some of the ranchers around here and put together cattle sales catalogs for a man out of Ranger and another fella out of San Angelo. It keeps me busy."

"Sounds like it. Do you enjoy what you do?"

She smiled, looking toward Joshua, who was wide awake and infatuated with the ceiling of the truck. "Most of the time."

"I know what you mean."

She turned toward him and Cort glanced her way. She had a curious expectant expression.

"I figured you loved what you do," she said. "I mean those are beautiful horses you have at your ranch. And you go to all those competitions. You see all those exciting places."

Cort glanced at her again. Did he hear longing in her voice? "Going to all those places alone isn't what it's cut out to be."

He studied the road, thinking. "I enjoy the training. But…I don't know. I guess I'm getting older. I'd rather stay home and let someone else hit the circuit rather than spend another night in a hotel room by myself."

Lilly probably thought he was some bleeding heart now. He realized it was true, though. After Ramona left him, he'd thrown himself into his work. But being on the road reminded him of everything he'd lost. Not that Ramona had enjoyed going with him. She hadn't, and when she did go, it was because of who she was going to get to rub elbows with. Famous people sank huge amounts of money into the horse industry. Ramona had loved the social aspect. She'd never really gone just to spend time with him.

He should have taken that as a hint that all was not right in his supposedly happy home.

"I'd love to go," Lilly said, surprising him. "I mean, not with you. I mean…well, what I'm trying to say is that I've been on the farm all my life. Being raised out there with my grannies was a very secluded upbringing. Granny Bunches used to always tell me that I should sell the farm when they were all dead and gone and head out to see the country. Of course, Mule Hollow is all I've ever known. And I love it…."

Her voice trailed off and Cort found himself studying her again. She was looking out the window, a frown creasing her face.

He wondered what it would be like to show her his world. To see his life through new eyes. Lilly's eyes.

It was a dangerous thing to wonder about.

"He weighs eleven pounds, and the doctor said it was all right for me to mix a bit of cereal in with his formula if he's been that sleepless." Lilly hadn't stopped talking since she'd come out of the doctor's office. "Thank goodness he's an older man, because I don't think the younger doctors would ever agree to such a thing." She was so excited to think about getting some sleep and to realize that her giving Joshua the cereal early wasn't bad. She couldn't contain her excitement.

Not to mention the fact that she was enjoying spending time with Cort.

They were sitting at a restaurant near the doctor's office. Lilly hadn't been out to eat in a real restaurant in ages. Cort had insisted on taking her to this nice steak house when she'd suggested a hamburger place out on the highway on their way home.

Cort seemed to get joy from making her feel special. He'd opened every door for her, carried Joshua and even held her elbow as she sat in the chair he'd pulled out for her. What a man. Not that there weren't men out there who did those things. There just had never been one who did them for her. Of course, she'd dated all of three people in her life.

Not that this was a date…oh, no, she knew better than that. Cort was just her neighbor. No matter how nice he'd been last night and today she couldn't forget that he'd made himself quite clear at the church on not being the right man for her. He wasn't interested in dating her. He was just being a nice neighbor.

She was on dangerous ground letting herself acknowledge everything about Cort that made her heart go thump.

Last night as she watched him drive away she'd wondered about his past. His wife had hurt him. He must have loved her very much to close himself off now and hide behind that grim expression—which had been fading more and more. Why, he actually cooed at Joshua as he'd taken him out of the car earlier. She wondered about that, too. The way he appeared to want to play with Joshua, to open up to the baby, but instead seemed to fight letting himself have free rein. It hit Lilly that Joshua would be very good for Cort. The plan she'd been toying with didn't seem quite so far-fetched anymore. Actually, it might be the best thing for Cort. And she did want to help him. He had been so good to her and her child. Even if he didn't think he was the right man for her…

She smiled, turning the plan over in her mind. Yes, her son needed a father figure, and Cort had been there for them during the delivery and lived right down the road. It was as if God had placed him there—not to help them as she'd first thought, but for them to help him.

Yes, that just might be it. God worked in very mysterious ways.

Cort ordered a steak, medium rare, and balked when she ordered hers well-done with a bottle of ketchup on the side.

"I know," she said, laughing. "I'm a Texas girl, so what am I doing eating a well-done steak?"

"You live in cattle country. You know you can't get the true taste of the meat when you burn it up like that," he teased.

"Can't help it. I eat ketchup on everything. You put it in my eggs the other night, so I know you like it, too. And I want my steak cooked. That's the flavor I like."

"The flavor of shoe leather."

"That's a matter of opinion. It's all about the texture."

"Yeah, but…okay, we'll agree to disagree about the texture of our steaks. What do you say?"

Lilly chuckled. "I say sounds like a plan to me."

When the waiter brought their plates twenty minutes later Lilly and Cort had laughed and disagreed on all manner of food preparation. Cort liked cold spinach out of the can, Lilly didn't touch the green stuff—despite the never-ending effort on the part of the grannies to stuff the nasty plant into all manner of food. Cort liked peanut butter on an apple, Lilly liked banana and peanut butter squashed together in a sandwich. Cort said he couldn't look at the stuff because it looked nasty all squashed together, much less eat it. To each his own,

Lilly thought. She knew he was missing out on one of life's premier foods.

They agreed on one thing: banana Laffy Taffy.

"If I had to choose one food to have on a deserted island with me it would be banana taffy," Lilly commented as the waiter set her steak down in front of her.

Cort laughed. "I love the stuff, but I might have to choose something else in that situation."

"Have it your way, but we only live once."

Cort just shook his head and began preparing his steak.

"Why, you sneak," she said as he opened the ketchup and bathed his steak in it. Looking up through a loose strand of black hair, he grinned sheepishly.

"I said nothin' about the ketchup. We were talking about the texture."

Lilly laughed. She couldn't remember the last time she'd had so much fun. Cort was a great guy.

Yep, she was certain the grannies would have changed their view of men if they'd known Cort.

At this point, Lilly really didn't care what the grannies thought.

Chapter Nineteen

Lilly sat beside the window and gazed out across the lawn and into the pasture that stretched as far as she could see. Samantha was ambling about munching stalks of grass peeking up through the cold earth. The little dear had stuck close to the house for the past few days, always coming to the living-room window and looking in at her as she and Joshua sat in the rocking chair.

Lilly enjoyed rocking Joshua and staring out the window. As she sang lullabies to him she imagined spending time with him there in the yard, seeing the seasons pass as she held her child. It was a wonderful feeling…this feeling of not being alone anymore. Of having someone to love, to watch over. She'd also taken up reading her Bible to him. With Joshua's birth, a new sense of meaning had taken over when she realized she was responsible to God to raise her baby in a manner that God would approve.

Joshua was sleeping contentedly, and Lilly had risen early to have quiet time with the Lord. Her Bible lay open in her lap. The verses she'd read filled her with hope.

Oh, there was so much to learn. Sure, her grandmothers—at least, Granny Bunches—had taken her to church and shown her that God loved her. But she had realized long ago that Granny Shu-Shu and Granny Gab had had a tilted view of the world in general, including God.

It wasn't as if they hadn't known the Lord, but they hadn't walked with Him. Granny Bunches, in her soft sweet way, had never condemned the views of her mother and sister, but she had tried to show Lilly another way. A loving way. Lilly had prayed this morning that God would help her to focus on the teachings in the Bible and the loving things Granny Bunches had shown her, instead of the negative thoughts and ways that the grannies Shu-Shu and Gab had drilled into her day after day.

Just like the traditions she wanted to start setting in place in Joshua's life, she had come to the understanding that bringing him up in the knowledge and love of God was most important of all.

Sitting there in her quiet living room, with the soft rays of sunshine filtering through lace curtains that were ages old, Lilly felt something change in her heart.

Instead of the grannies' way, Lilly understood that it was time for her to find her own way.

And she wanted that to be God's way.

The air was brisk as Cort urged Ringo into a slow trot. The big horse was feeling frisky today. Beneath him Cort could feel the animal straining to move more quickly, anxious to feel the freedom that came with the release of pent-up energy. Cort gave the familiar cluck with his mouth, and the big horse expanded into a lope around the round pen. Cort tried to concentrate on the exercise at hand, but his mind was not on the horse.

It was on Lilly.

For days he'd let his guard down, tried to pretend that she could remain just a friend. But he was fooling himself. He had been from the first moment he'd looked at her. Lilly was a woman with whom a man could build a future. She was outspoken, but tender. She'd had her heart broken and her dreams dismissed, but she'd managed to hold on to her optimism.

She was a wonderful mother. Every time she and Joshua were near him, he had to fight the want that filled him. He loved—no, he wouldn't go there. He couldn't allow himself to acknowledge the feelings that had set up camp in his soul.

They'd sat together at church again. Her sitting next to him, as Pastor Lewis talked about God's plan for the family, seemed almost like a cruel joke. But he knew the messages were meant for the single men in the congregation who were vested in finding a wife and growing a family. Pastor Lewis was laying the groundwork for Christian men to become Christian husbands and fathers. Mule Hollow wanted to grow and become a thriving small community, and the majority of those wanting this plan to succeed were men seeking God's will for their lives.

Lilly would one day belong with one of them.

And Cort would just have to pray for grace to be able to watch her find the love she deserved.

"Hey, Loser," Lilly called, hating the name. The sulking dog saw her coming up the drive, lifted his scraggly head, then hopped from the porch and wiggled all the way to meet her.

"We've got to give you a new name." He lapped up

the attention with every fiber of his hairy body. Cort had told her more than once that Loser had started living after he'd met her and Samantha.

The idea gave Lilly a warm fuzzy feeling. But it was time to do what she'd come to do, so she sucked in a fortifying breath and said another prayer, then looked around.

"Where's Cort?" she asked, supporting the sling that held Joshua against her as she scratched Loser between the eyes. He looked up at her with a big foolish grin on his face, but didn't answer. So she had to rely on her ears and the clanking noise coming from the barn.

She found Cort on the ground under a tractor. His long legs stuck out from beneath the large machine.

"Hey, neighbor, got a problem?" she asked, stooping so that she could peer under at what he was doing.

His hands were covered in grease, and when he looked at her she could see there was a streak of black running across one cheek. His eyes brightened when he saw her. And Lilly's heart faltered, then picked up a quicker pace. Even the two mile walk from her house hadn't caused her heart to pound as it was doing now. This erratic beating was a feeling she'd come to understand only Cort's presence could produce.

"Nothing I can't handle," he said, scooting from beneath the tractor to face her.

They were only inches apart, and Lilly, without thinking, reached to pull a cobweb from just above Cort's ear. Her fingers froze on contact with his silky hair.

Cort's gaze locked with hers and she yanked her hand back, feeling at odds with their closeness. Wanting it, yet fearing it.

Only after she was stroking Joshua's hair could she speak. "I came to ask you something." Her voice wobbled.

With a power she didn't know she possessed, she forced down the fear overcoming her from the inside out and looked at Cort. He hadn't moved. He sat in exactly the same position as when she'd reached out and touched him. His eyes drilled into hers. The intensity threatened her willpower and almost loosened the unknown, unexplored feelings she was struggling frantically to file away until later.

Later, when she was alone, when it might be safe to really look inside her heart.

Not being able to take the proximity any longer, she crossed the room to sit on a hay bale.

The day was cold, but the sun had been shining during her brisk walk and had kept her warm. Now, in the shadow of the barn, the chill swept over her and she pulled the blanket more securely around Joshua. She knew the baby sling that strapped him to her surrounded him with her body heat. He was as cozy as a bug in a rug, as her Granny Gab would've said. But she needed something to occupy her hands, and fidgeting with the blanket fulfilled that need. When she looked up, Cort was on his feet wiping his hands and face with a rag. He had his back to her, giving her a moment to take a deep breath.

This was crazy!

Calm down, Lilly. This is what God has been leading you to do! "I've been thinking. And, well, you see…I was wondering. No, I was wanting to ask you—" As she faltered he turned toward her, his sweet face full of bewilderment.

This is right. Ask him. "I've been reading my Bible. And I was reading about when Hannah gave her baby Samuel back to the Lord, she actually said she lent him back to the Lord because the Lord had blessed her with him. I want to honor the Lord for blessing me with Joshua by promising the Lord that I'll raise him up in a godly home."

Cort raised an eyebrow, but didn't smile. "I think that's a great thing to do."

He had finished wiping his hands, and he came to. lean against the stall railing a few feet away from Lilly. He tucked his fingers inside the top of his pocket and studied her.

He looked so strong and handsome. Lilly tugged at the collar of her coat and tried not to think about how his arms felt around her, or how safe she felt in them.

"Parenthood is serious business. Raising children God's way is the greatest, most rewarding thing a parent can do."

Cort paused, and Lilly wondered at the sadness that flickered in his expressive eyes. Had he wanted to do the same thing for his children? Children he now understood he would never father? Lilly's heart ached. Cort would have made a wonderful father. Of this she was certain. This gave her courage to continue. If he denied her request, then at least she'd asked.

"I want to make this promise to the Lord in the sanctuary and I also wanted to ask you something. I know this is a lot of responsibility…that maybe with your business and your life you might want to say no. And I would understand. Really." *Out with it, Lilly!* "Would you be Joshua's guardian, godparent…if something were to happen to me?"

Cort's head swung up from where he'd been studying his boots. His expression was blank. His jaw dropped.

Good or bad, she couldn't tell.

"I mean, you did rescue us both. You are the reason

he's okay." The light that had flickered in his eyes died, and Lilly fought to get it back when he didn't answer as he studied Joshua, a sad quirk turning the edge of his mouth down.

"And you would be such a good father to him…if, if something were to happen to me." There, she'd said it all.

Cort met her gaze and for a long moment neither of them moved. Or breathed.

"Nothing's going to happen to you, Lilly."

"I don't know that." Now that she'd spoken the words she knew the importance of them. Knew she was right. Knew in her heart he was the one to fill the spot, should something go wrong and God called her home.

"Even if something did happen there are plenty of others who would be happy to raise Joshua. I'm sure Lacy and Clint would love to be his godparents. They'd be better than an old single guy like me."

"They would be wonderful. I know that. But you have a bond with him. And you are not old."

"Lacy has a bond. She delivered him."

Lilly reached out and laid her hand on his forearm. His muscles tensed beneath her fingers. "But you got him there. You came through the night and carried us to safety. You're the one God sent to take care of us."

Cort thought for a long moment and Lilly's heart sank. She knew he didn't want her, but she'd hoped that he would want Joshua.

"I'll be his godparent."

Lilly didn't know if she should be happy or sad at the tone of his voice. But then again, she'd known getting him to say yes would be like splitting logs with a rubber ax.

"I would be honored to take the responsibility that goes with the request."

Okay, so that sounded better. A tremor raced up the base of her spine and Lilly stood on shaking legs. "Thank you."

Tears of relief suddenly stung her eyes, and before she could help it, one slipped from the corner, trailing down her cheek. She dashed it away with her hand and turned to go. Her emotions seemed to be sitting on her shoulder these days. Thing was, she really didn't understand what was wrong. She couldn't blame her wobbly emotions on lack of sleep anymore.

Cort's hand on her shoulder stopped her.

"Lilly, don't cry. Nothing's going to happen to you." Cort gently turned her toward him and wrapped his arms around her, tenderly cupping Joshua between them. She melted.

Home.

The word swelled in her heart. Suddenly she knew the truth. She'd tried to deny it. Tried to overcome it. But in her heart of hearts she knew in the circle of Cort's arms she'd found her place.

"And with the rib, which the Lord God had taken from man, made He a woman, and brought her unto the man."

The familiar verse from second Genesis sprang out at her, surrounded her and she knew…

She knew she'd found the man God had intended her for.

Cort tightened his arms around Lilly and cherished the feeling of her and her child next to him. Waves of regret washed over him for a lost past and a future he could never have. But he could give her what she asked, knowing that he would do anything needed to make her life and Joshua's easier.

He didn't want to see her cry. Looking down, he

tilted her chin toward him and looked into the shining gold of her eyes. When her lip trembled and her eyes misted, he kissed her.

He'd meant only to hold her, to console her, but his heart got in the way, and the need to acknowledge his love for her overwhelmed him.

He did love her. He'd loved her from the first moment he'd seen her lying on the floor of his barn with that unbelievable bright smile spread across her lovely face. She had an undaunted spirit. One even a lasso couldn't hinder.

But she can't be yours.

The cruel truth hissed through him. It took everything he had to pull away from her. She had accepted the kiss with warmth and returned it with a sweetness that broke his heart.

"This," he said as he rammed a hand through his hair and tried not to heed the questions in her eyes, "isn't a good idea. It wouldn't work."

"Why not?" she asked. Her voice was soft. A whisper. Her eyes were dark with emotion. "I know I'm not your wife. But—"

"It hasn't a thing to do with Ramona. That's over. It's about you. You and Joshua. You need more than I can give you. You *deserve* more."

Lilly straightened. "I think you don't give yourself enough credit. And I know you don't give me enough."

"It's not about giving myself credit. It's about you having the family that I know God has in store for you."

Lilly's eyes flashed. "How do you know what God has in store for me? Who are you to say it isn't with you?" She stopped, and the silence stretched between.

Cort didn't want to hurt her, but he knew this was for the best. Now he wasn't certain if agreeing to be

Joshua's guardian had been the right choice. When she remarried, there would be a man in Josh's life. They wouldn't need him anymore.

"God has a husband out there for you and a father for Joshua. But it isn't me, Lilly. I have nothing to offer you. So the best thing would be for us to forget this ever happened."

The fire that flashed through Lilly's eyes took him by surprise. And his mouth dropped when she stepped away from him, plopped her hand on her narrow hip, cupped Joshua with the other hand and glared sassily up at him. "Well, cowboy, you can forget it if you want to, but *I* don't want to."

And with that she turned and flounced away, curls bouncing. With Loser trailing behind her.

Chapter Twenty

The town was in an uproar. The ladies had gotten together and planned Lacy's wedding down to the last pink imported Shasta daisy.

Bless her soon-to-be-husband's big heart, Clint had given in to them plain and simply because he loved Lacy. Loved her with a love that Lilly could only wish to find. A love that she, in her own misguided way, had thought she'd found. But she'd been wrong.

Cort hadn't come after her.

Today Adela was watching Joshua while Lilly had a day out with Lacy. Lilly wanted her son to know the love of Adela, Norma Sue and Esther Mae. She wanted to encourage their bonding. Because of this she had agreed to the plan to get her out of the house and help with the final stages of Lacy's wedding.

Standing in the back of the church watching Lacy and Ashby Templeton discuss flowers, Lilly bowed her head and prayed that God would sustain her, that He would give her the strength she needed to do what He wanted her to do. It was a hard prayer to pray. Given the nature

of her outspoken personality, she wanted to demand
that Cort acknowledge that he loved her.

She needed Cort. Him and Joshua. And God. What
a blessing that circle of love could be. But she didn't
allow herself to demand such a thing because she didn't
know if it was true.

Why would she even think that? Cort had never told
her anything remotely close to admitting he loved her.
Yes, he'd shown her care and friendship and kindness.
But love? No. He'd flat-out told her that he wasn't the
man for her. They'd hardly had anything remotely close
to a romantic relationship. Sure, they'd shared one kiss.
One tender big kiss. And then he'd run for the hills!
Really, Lilly didn't understand why in the world she'd
expected him to feel more. Who was she kidding?

Watching Lacy as she talked, Lilly smiled, despite
the misery she felt inside. The crazy girl wouldn't stop
babbling. It was as if she knew something was wrong,
but she hadn't asked. She'd simply drawn Lilly into the
final plans for her wedding with a great smile and a host
of enthusiasm. Of course, this was Lacy, and she'd ef-
ficiently involved everyone. A Valentine's Day wedding
in Mule Hollow was appropriate.

Molly had been writing articles about Mule Hollow
every so often in her column for the paper in Houston
and there were a few other big papers that were picking
up the stories. Why, even a New York paper had picked
up on them. They were a big hit with Molly's reader-
ship. The very first wedding for the town that had con-
ducted a national "wives needed" ad campaign was big
news…at least to the growing army of faithful readers.
The fact that the campaign had actually produced a
marriage within the first six months was huge. It made

women realize that this wasn't just a publicity stunt. It made them actually see that they could have a future in Mule Hollow.

"Lilly," Lacy said, plopping down in the pew beside her. Ashby settled into the one in front of them. "What do you think about pink baby roses and pink—"

"Sounds like a scene from *Steel Magnolias*," Lilly said, cringing.

"I loved that movie," Lacy gushed. "Julia Roberts walking down the aisle with an ocean of pink around her—it was great. Why, the first time I saw that movie, I knew if I ever got married I wanted that same sea of flowers around me." She was nodding her head and looking about the church. "Yep, yep, yep…I can just see it."

Ashby's gaze met Lilly's and they both burst out laughing. If there was one thing Lacy Brown loved it was pink. She studied them both as they subsided into a fit of giggles.

"I'm telling you, it'll be beautiful. Remember, it's Valentine's Day. Pink or red is the only way to go. And as you know, I'm a pink kinda girl."

Lilly straightened her face, keeping her eyes off Ashby lest they start chuckling again. "Lacy, it's your wedding, and if you want the walls pink, it would be fine with me. It's going to be beautiful no matter what. And you're right—pink on Valentine's will be perfect. But please tell me you aren't having Clint wear pink, are you?"

Lacy smiled. "He loves me, but that would be pushing things a bit. Gray and black mix quite nicely with pink. I'm not wearing pink, so I couldn't ask him to."

"You didn't really think about asking him such a thing, did you?" Ashby asked, not certain when to take Lacy seriously and when not to.

"No. I didn't even think about it. Clint's a cowboy. Besides, he already wore pink once because of me. And he didn't like it one bit."

Lilly smiled, remembering the story of Clint getting an entire bucket of hot pink paint dumped on his head the day Lacy was painting her salon. The story was one she didn't think he would ever live down. But he'd handled it good-naturedly. He'd said it didn't matter what happened to him as long as he got Lacy in the end.

Lilly's heart twisted, thinking about Cort. She felt the same way about him. Anything was worth it, if she could have his love at the end of the day.

If only she could figure a way.

Leave it in God's hands, Lilly.

Sometimes it was easier to think something than to actually do it. She had to remind herself that God had big hands.

And that those big hands would take care of her no matter what.

After they'd finished at the church Ashby left them to take care of ordering the flowers. She had a contact in Hollywood—her former home—who was shipping the flowers out to Mule Hollow by Friday morning. Actually she was shipping herself out with them. And if Ashby had her way she was going to stay and run her Internet flower business from Mule Hollow. It was going to be one more opportunity for the little town. E-commerce was making possible several things that ten years ago wouldn't have been imaginable. Ashby's mail-order dress business was running as smoothly from Mule Hollow as it had from Hollywood. The dresses she'd helped everyone order for the wedding were gorgeous.

Lilly and Lacy then hopped into Lacy's 1958 pink Cadillac convertible, with the top up and the heater on, and headed for the community center, where the reception was going to be held. With the wedding only a week away, the decorating was already in progress. Today they were going to help put up white and pink netting along with fairy lights.

The scenery was whizzing past the Caddy's windows as Lilly relaxed in the deep seat.

"I just love to drive," Lacy said, sitting up straight, watching the road as she maneuvered the huge car down the blacktop. "I especially like to ride with the top down. Do you mind if I put it down?"

Lilly shot an unbelieving glance at Lacy. "It's forty-five degrees outside."

"Have you ever ridden in a convertible with the top down on a forty-degree day?" She glanced at Lilly with an excited grin and a raised eyebrow.

"Well, no. But it's cold."

"Girl, you need to live a little. Before we go to the community center, we are going for a ride. Because you need to tell me what ails you."

Lacy slammed on the brakes and the Caddy skidded to a halt. Before Lilly could overcome the shock of the sudden stop she watched in horror as Lacy pressed a button and the Caddy's top kicked into gear. The cold of the day whipped into the car just as Lacy stomped on the accelerator. Flattened to the seat from the speed, Lilly felt her curls rise and start dancing above her head as if they were alive. The brisk cold stung her cheeks and the chilly air sucked a laugh right out of her. Lacy was laughing, too.

Lacy turned up the heat, and suddenly Lilly had the

best of both worlds. She was warm, her feet were toasty and her hands, too, but the cold air on her face, blowing through her hair, sent a thrill of joy pulsing through her.

"I told you it was great," Lacy yelled over the wind as she whipped the car onto another farm road heading away from town.

"I love it. I could get used to this. Is this car for sale?" Lilly called out, knowing full well that Lacy would never part with her beloved car.

"Nope, nope, never. But I know where you could get one just like it."

Lilly considered it. She did need a new car, but she needed a family car. One she could feel safe in on the road with Joshua. "I guess I'd better pass. But I'm going to be asking for a ride in this one more often. Now that you have me hooked."

"That I can do." Lacy slowed the Caddy and pulled the car over next to a deserted one-picnic-table rest area. "Okay, so now that I have you loosened up, tell me how things are going. God has really put you on my mind lately."

Lilly could hear the sincerity in Lacy's voice and she could see it in her eyes. In the short time she'd known Lacy her enthusiasm and love for God had inspired Lilly. She was bold for Christ and humble in her accomplishments for Him. Lilly knew she wanted to be like Lacy…in her own way. No one could be like Lacy—she was truly one of a kind. But Lilly could learn from her and she could trust her.

Sitting there in the cold air, Lilly felt comfortable enough to let Lacy inside her heart. "I married Jeff because I was lonely and to disprove the legacy my grannies tried to pass down to me. I made a bad choice."

Lilly studied the landscape, the barren pastures waiting for spring. "It was a huge mistake. After he left me, after I started coming back to church, after I met you, I realized that I hadn't waited on the Lord. I tried to hate Jeff. But I couldn't. Jeff didn't know the Lord. He didn't care or understand that marriage is a commitment made before God. I let my wanting a husband get ahead of waiting on the one God had in mind for me. Do you think I'm right about that?"

Lacy paused for a few moments. "I can't say what God's mind was then. I'm sure He wanted you to do what you could to make the marriage work once you had committed to Jeff. But he left and it's over. You understand the concept—one man, one woman for as long as the two shall live."

Lilly nodded. "Yes."

Lacy reached over and placed a cold hand on Lilly's. "Do you still want a husband?"

"Yes. Yes, I do. Despite my grandmothers, I want to have a family. I look at Joshua and every negative thing my grannies said about marriage, about men, all of it just disappears into thin air. I want a husband. And I want more children. But I don't want just any husband. I want Cort."

Lacy smiled. "I thought so! I told you I thought he was your future."

"But Lacy, he doesn't want to marry me, for reasons I'm not at liberty to talk about."

"Do you love him?"

Lilly looked at her hands. "Yes, yes I do."

"Do you trust God?"

Lilly looked at Lacy. Her blond hair looked like whipped cream after a pie-smashing contest, but the wisdom that shone from her blue eyes reached far into Lilly's heart. "I want to trust Him."

"I was reading a verse this morning. 'Commit thy way unto the Lord; trust also in Him; and He shall bring it to pass.' I believe that was Psalm 37:4." Lacy thought for a second. "Nope, it was 37:5 because verse four is, I remember now, 'Delight thyself also in the Lord; and He shall give thee the desires of thine heart.'"

Lacy searched Lilly's eyes with hers as Lilly pondered the verses. Commit her way unto the Lord. That was what had been on her mind lately. She hadn't done that— at least, she hadn't tried to do that until recently. And she hadn't totally committed to it until she'd looked into the face of Joshua. "I want my child to know that his mother loves the Lord. My delight would be that he grow to know the Lord. That he join me in heaven one day. That he grow up to be a man of God. And I would like him to have the guidance of a father in his life."

"Are you prepared to wait on the Lord?"

The question shocked Lilly. She had been all set to go after Cort. To convince him that he was the man for her. But was she prepared to wait on the Lord? Was she once more trying to rush the plan that God had for her life? Lilly sat up straight and gawked at Lacy. "How in the world did you get to be so smart?"

Lacy laughed. "Oh, Lilly, it isn't me. God prepared my heart for this conversation. I prayed this morning that whatever it was that was bothering you, He would speak through me. That He would just kick me to the curb and use my big mouth to speak to you."

Lilly lowered her head and stared at her hands folded in her lap. "Yes, I'm prepared to wait on the Lord. Only He could have known what I needed to hear."

Lacy squeezed Lilly's shoulder. "God wants what's best for you and Joshua, Lilly. But whatever is going on may not be about you. It could be about Cort. Give it time and pray. God has a plan. And I have faith that whatever it is, it's gonna be wonderful. And it's gonna outshine anything you could imagine."

"But what if He doesn't give me Cort? How can I go on?"

"God's grace is sufficient to sustain you through anything. He promises that. He doesn't say His grace *might* be sufficient. He says His grace *is* sufficient. Things in this life hurt. You've already learned that. Life isn't fair. Satan is alive and well and striking out at every turn. But I know that when my dad left me and my mom, when he turned his back on us, it hurt so much. But God carried me through. He was faithful and I've used that pain to counsel many other people with similar problems because I understood what they were going through. He will carry you, Lilly. He will carry you every step of the way if you need Him to. But I know you. I saw in you a spirit, the first time I saw you singing in the church choir. Like this town, you have a spirit that wants to soar for God. You just have to trust Him. Act out on that trust and pass on His grace as the opportunity arises. You're going to be all right, Lilly Tipps."

Lilly reached over and hugged Lacy. "Thank you, Lacy. God blessed me the day you became my friend."

Lacy gave her a hard squeeze. "Girl, I can't even begin to list all the blessings He's given me. But you are one of them. And that Clint Matlock, bless his sweet soul, is the icing on my cake. And I wasn't even looking for him when God put him in my path." She released

Lilly, put the car in gear, then gunned the engine, smiling big-time at the loud sound.

Lilly sucked in a breath and held on as they shot out onto the blacktop heading back toward town.

"You get ready, Lilly," Lacy called out like a cheerleader. "Because our God is an *awesome* God and there is truly no telling what's going to happen next for you and Joshua. No telling at all."

Lilly couldn't help but smile.

Even when a bug hit her between the eyes.

Chapter Twenty-One

Cort put the screwdriver back into his toolbox, then closed the door to the feed room and tried out the freshly relocated bolt near the top of the door. No way would Samantha get into the feed room now. He felt a bit guilty for having changed the lock. What would Samantha think, after having been allowed in the room all her life, to now being ousted?

She was just a donkey. A little pesky burro. But she seemed like more. He had grown attached to the old girl. Just as he'd grown attached to Lilly. And Joshua.

Loser was sitting at his feet. He wasn't lying at his feet—he was actually sitting there. At attention. Why, the dog even wagged his tail every once in a while. And if Cort even got near his truck, the crazy animal would run and leap into the truck bed and look expectantly at him. Loser wanted to go, but not just anywhere. Loser wanted to see Samantha. Cort felt the same way about Lilly. He wanted to get in his truck every time he passed by and drive over to see what was going on at the end of the dirt road.

But he couldn't do it. He'd kissed Lilly. Then he'd

told her he wasn't the man for her. He'd turned the sweet woman away when, in his heart, he'd wanted nothing more than to hang on to her with both hands and never let her go.

He'd misled her.

And he'd hurt her.

But there was nothing he could do about it. He was learning the hard way that life wasn't fair, and it definitely didn't care how many times it struck him down.

When Ramona left he'd not been able to blame her. She wanted children. She'd always wanted them, and no matter how much it had hurt Cort to watch her leave, he'd understood deep inside that he had to let her go. It was for her best interests. Letting Lilly go was for her best interests, also. He just couldn't believe that God would lead him all the way out into the middle of nowhere just to dangle Lilly in front of him. But then, he hadn't understood much the Lord had been up to lately.

He looked over at the now almost smiling Loser.

"Well, I'm glad one of us is happy. I feel like God's put me on a merry-go-round. Only, there isn't anything merry about it. It's just one stinking heartache after another."

Loser tilted his head and barked, then ran over to the truck that sat at the end of the barn. He wiggled his body like a dust mop being beaten against a rug. The closer Cort got to the truck the wilder and more erratic his wiggling became.

"I'm not going over there, Loser. That's the last place I need to be." He looked at his watch and saw that it was nearing three o'clock. He had promised Clint he'd help him and a bunch of the other cowboys set up a few more tables for the wedding that was to take place on Saturday.

Chapter Twenty-Two

❧

"Lacy Brown, get away from that door."

Lacy ignored Norma Sue and continued to peek through the heavy door of the church. "It's packed!"

Lilly chuckled. Despite her heavy heart she was determined to enjoy Lacy's wedding. And so was Lacy. Lilly stood on tiptoes and peeked over Lacy's head. The little sanctuary was filled with all kinds of cowboys and a good many women. Some of them she recognized as having come to the dinner theater.

"You see anybody out there making eyes at each other?" Esther Mae asked, bumping into Lacy and then Lilly as she tried to get an eyeball to the crack in the door.

"Esther, watch it," Norma snapped. "Your big feet are steppin' on Lacy's dress." Lilly was glad Adela was playing the piano loudly, so it would drown out all the chattering.

"Norma, Norma, Norma, calm down," Lacy said with a laugh. "Look out there. Look how beautiful and happy Clint's mother looks. I'm so glad she came to the wedding and that she and Clint are getting to know each other again."

Lilly could see Clint's mother in the second row beside Lacy's mother. It was hard to believe, looking at her, that she'd run off with a man from the circus when Clint was just a boy. But she'd recently become a Christian and asked for Clint's forgiveness. Now here she was about to witness her son's marriage. God was incredible. He'd restored a family after years of separation. It did her heart good to know God's faithfulness.

Lilly thought of Joshua, and of Cort. Would God bring them all together as a family? Lilly had been praying for the Lord's will to be done in her life. And yet the moment Cort had walked into the church her stomach had started churning and her pulse had increased. Cort Wells made her happy even from a distance.

"Oh, and look at Molly taking all those pictures," Lacy hissed in an excited whisper, reeling in Lilly's runaway thoughts. "There's Cort sitting by Sheriff Brady. Lilly, just wait till he sees you in that dress. Oh, Molly just took their picture."

Lilly glanced down at the ice-pink dress she wore. She still couldn't believe she was one of Lacy's bridesmaids. Of course, Lacy was different. She'd wanted Norma Sue, Esther Mae and Adela to also be her bridesmaids, but they'd refused, declaring they were way too old. In the end she had her roommate, Sherri, as her maid of honor and Lilly as her bridesmaid.

Esther Mae and Norma Sue were watching Joshua for her.

"Okay, ladies," Ashby said from behind them. Everyone spun around, bumping elbows as they lined up in front of her. She was the acting wedding planner, and she looked the part in her elegant suit and silky straight hair.

"My, my, but all of you look like you've had your hands in the candy jar. What's going on?"

"We're just people watching," Norma Sue said, jiggling Joshua in her arms.

"Well, it's about time for you to march down the aisle."

Lilly was more nervous than Lacy. When the wedding march started Lilly was in place only because Ashby set her there and gave her a tiny nudge that it was time for her to get things rolling. She wanted to roll, all right. Right out the door.

Everyone in the church turned, watching her, but her feet wouldn't move.

"Go," Ashby whispered from behind the door. Sucking in a deep breath that immediately stuck in her lungs, Lilly stepped out.

Cort was sitting in the second row from the back, and his eyes caught hers. She was finally able to breathe again when she reached the front of the church and took her appointed spot.

In her mind's eye she could see Cort, standing where Clint stood waiting for his bride.

And Lilly wanted it to be her.

She so wanted it to be her.

Please, Lord, give me peace. Help me be satisfied with Your plan for my life.

Cort had watched Lilly walk slowly down the aisle. Her curls were swept up on top of her head in a pleasing mass of disarray that exposed her smooth neck. Her barely pink dress contrasted with the warmth of her eyes. When their eyes met she'd looked away, toward the front of the church. Cort hadn't been able to tear his gaze away, following her every step.

And he noticed his weren't the only eyes that appreciated the picture of beauty Lilly made as she took her place at the front of the church. Cort was sitting near the back, and out of the corner of his eye he could see Bob Jacobs. He stood tall and straight in his tuxedo. He was, Cort felt sure, what a woman would find handsome in a man. And he watched every move Lilly made.

Sherri passed him on her way to stand in the maid-of-honor spot and Cort didn't even notice, he was so caught up in thinking about Lilly and Bob. One second Lilly stood there alone, then Sherri took her place beside her. Sherri was beautiful, too. Her normally crazy Rod Stewart hair was curled softly about her face, taking away the radical look she was known for and exposing a more vulnerable woman. But Cort had eyes only for Lilly. She was everything he wanted.

And there lay his problem. Nothing about it had changed since the first night he'd met her. He needed that kick in the head, and he needed it badly.

When he finally focused on the wedding, Lacy and Clint were beaming at each other as Pastor Lewis asked each of them if they'd take the other in sickness and in health, for richer or for poorer, in good times and in bad times. When Lacy reached out and cupped Clint's jaw as she said "I do," Cort's eyes again sought out Lilly.

There were tears in her eyes and a sad smile on her lips.

His heart ached. He wanted the best for Lilly. She deserved it.

It didn't matter that all he really wanted to do was walk to the front of that church, take her in his arms and ask her to be his. All that mattered was that Lilly get the family she deserved.

Trust me.

The words of the Lord came to Cort as he watched Lilly's lip tremble. Why was she near tears? His chest tightened and his fist knotted tightly.

Lilly needed whatever the Lord had in store for her. Once more he reminded himself of this. *Trust me.* Wasn't that what he'd felt God telling him this morning when he'd opened his Bible looking for answers? All day he'd meditated on the words. Was he trusting God? Did he believe that God had a plan?

Did he?

The answer was yes.

But watching Lilly, lovely Lilly, with her eyes glistening with tears and her lip trembling as she watched two people unite in marriage, he faltered. How was he to know if he should try for a future with Lilly or stay out of her way and simply be her friend?

Until he understood what God wanted from him he would stay out of her way. He would simply be there as her friend when she and Joshua needed him.

It felt wrong.

Every day it felt more wrong than the day before. Still, it remained the right thing to do.

Lilly stood on the front walk of the community center and studied the array of cars parked along Main Street. There had to be three hundred people here tonight. The inside of the building was bulging at the bricks with full capacity. Leave it to Lacy to make her reception a memorable one. Who but Lacy Brown would have a karaoke party for a reception? *An all-love-song karaoke bash!*

Bash was right. There were all kinds of love songs being butchered inside. While it was fun and hilarious at the same time, Lilly had needed to escape, to catch her breath and contain her nerves. Being near Cort—and yet his seeming so distant—hurt. He'd stayed across the room from her all night, talking with Roy Don and Hank.

Adela had taken Joshua home with her, saying she would leave the partying for the young adults. She was spending time with the youngster of Mule Hollow.

Now Lilly was torn between going to pick him up and heading home or going back inside. Cort continued to make it quite clear that he wasn't the one for her, that she needed a younger man who could give her children.

For the past week she'd tried to heed Lacy's advice and wait on the Lord. But it was so hard.

There was no way she could go over to Cort's without a good reason, as if she were throwing herself at him. No way would she ever do that again.

Lilly bit her lip thinking of the wedding. It had been wonderful, yet her emotions were bouncing around and the least little thing was making her want to cry.

And love songs were the pits!

Sure, if you were in love they were perfect! But for someone whose love life was crashing around her feet, listening to off-key renditions really hurt.

She wasn't in the best of moods, and it seemed as if God wasn't listening.

"Hey, Lilly, you are a definite knockout tonight."

Lilly glanced over at Bob as he walked out onto the front walk to stand beside her. His dimples were huge and his grin was sparkling in the fairy lights that hung along the porch.

"Thanks, Bob. It was Lacy who was the knockout." Lilly pushed away her mood and smiled at her new friend.

"Aren't you cold?" He rubbed his hands together, cocked his head to the side and eyed her suspiciously. "Something wrong?"

"No and no. No, I'm not cold, and no, nothing is wrong. I just needed a break from all the love songs."

Bob nodded and relaxed against the railing, turning so he could face her. "I know what you mean. That ceremony really made me think about the future. I'm ready for the Lord to send me a wife to settle down with on my own little piece of land."

"I'm sure God's going to send you a great wife. You're a wonderful guy."

It was starting to get cold to Lilly now and she suddenly felt awkward. "I guess I'd better go inside. The chill is setting in through my coat."

"Yeah, and I think Lacy is going to throw her flower thing in a few minutes. You might catch it."

"I'm not even going to try."

"Why not? You might be the next bride in Mule Hollow. Any man would be lucky to have you as a wife."

Lilly felt the sting of tears returning to the back of her eyes and she fought them off. "Any woman would be blessed to have you as a husband. Maybe you'd better get busy and pick one out."

Bob held the door open for her, grinning down at her as she walked back into the warm room. As she passed by him he leaned close and whispered in her ear. "Maybe *you* should get busy picking, too."

Lilly paused in the doorway and looked up into his smiling face. Was he flirting with her? When he winked, she blinked, feeling heat rising up her collar. They were just friends. Right? She hadn't done anything to make him think she was interested…had she?

"Some guys don't know what it is that they need."

Lilly didn't know what to say. She moved past him into the crowded room, pausing when he reached for her coat.

"I'll take this for you, Lilly. That way, you can go find Cort."

What? She swung around and met his twinkling eyes.

He tugged playfully at a ringlet dangling near her ear, then spoke so softly only she could hear. "Lilly, anybody can see you're in love with the guy. I was just teasing you because you're so cute when you're blushing. Now, give me your coat and go catch that bouquet of flowers when Lacy throws it."

Chapter Twenty-Three

"Nope, never did see anything quite like it," Applegate Thornton said, scratching his gray hair. His wrinkled face was scrunched up in a corkscrew grimace and frankly, Cort had never seen anything quite like *it* before.

It was six-thirty in the morning and Cort had come to Pete's feed store for, of all things, alfalfa. Samantha had stolen all of his, and Pete had informed him at the wedding that he'd finally gotten in a fresh supply. Since Cort hadn't been able to sleep, he'd decided to get a head start on the day by coming out first thing and picking it up.

He hadn't thought there would be a line.

Applegate Thornton and Stanley Orr had their morning checkers match over at Sam's Diner every daybreak until after nine. Once a week they came to Pete's for a new bag of sesame seeds. This morning Cort found himself behind them as Pete weighed and bagged the seeds, and then they weighed and balanced everything that had happened at the wedding reception Saturday night. Obviously a lot had happened after

Cort left, having listened to about all the love singing he could stomach for one evening.

Not that he didn't appreciate love. He did. But when a fella was in over his head, with weights on his ankles, the last thing he wanted to hear was the fifty greatest love songs sung by fifty not-so-great crooners. But that hadn't been what sent him packing. It hadn't even been when Applegate had decided to try his hand at singing a Beatles favorite.

Cort had left when he'd seen Bob whispering in Lilly's ear and watching the pretty shade of pink she turned and the adoring way she stared into the cowboy's eyes.

Needless to say, Cort hadn't slept a wink, and he hadn't slept well last night, either. His mood was about as dark as the night he'd barely made it through. And standing in line at the feed store wasn't improving his attitude one bit.

"Did you hear what I said?" Applegate leaned toward him, as if Cort was the one who couldn't hear, and repeated himself, louder this time. "I said, never did see anything quite like it."

"He heard ya the first time, App. He ain't hard a-hearin'. I am. And I heard ya the first time. You ignoring him, son?"

Cort stared from one man to the next. "I heard him the first time."

"Then you were ignorin' me." Applegate's expression grew dark, his bushy eyebrows met in the middle and his skin wrinkled up around his nose as his lips drooped.

"No, sir, I was not ignoring you."

"Did ya hear that, Stan—says he wasn't ignoring me. Pete, did ya hear that?"

Cort prayed for patience and tried to step to the counter, but the older man slapped him on his back and chuckled.

"I saw you sneak off before Lacy threw that boo-kay of flowers. You shoulda stayed. Your girlfriend was standing there, not looking too happy…. Did you think she was looking happy, Stan?"

"Nope, she looked like she wanted to be home long 'fore they threw that flower ball. Can't say I blame her. Poor thang."

Cort shifted from one boot to the other. He didn't want to hear any more about Lilly. She'd probably caught the bouquet and would be the next bride in Mule Hollow. She and Bob would make a great couple. They'd have a houseful of kids.

"Tell him what happened, App." Pete said, trying to get App to tell, or move, probably so the line would thin out and he could get back to warming his feet over by the stove Cort saw in the corner.

Cort scooted his hat back from his eyes and studied the older man. "Mr. Applegate, what was so bad about Saturday night?" He'd decided it was better to ask and get it over with rather than wait.

"Okay, so there your girlfriend stood all quiet like with all them other outsiders. Them women were huddled up in the corner like a bunch of running backs going out for a pass. Lacy chucked the flowers, and I'm telling you they were heading straight for your girlfriend—"

"She isn't my girlfriend," Cort interrupted—to the wind, because Applegate kept right on going.

"We were all holding our breath that Lilly was going to raise her hands, so the ball of flowers wouldn't give her a black eye or anything, and all of a sudden like Michael Jordan getting hang time, football and basketball collided, along with a couple of them women. Right there in the building. This ole gal rose into the air in a dive that lasted all of ten minutes in slow motion. Yes, sir, that gal hung in the air with one arm out ahead of her and she snatched that bunch of flowers right before they hit Lilly. Onliest problem was, another of them gals was hangin' ten coming from the other direction."

Applegate rubbed his chin with two fingers and studied Cort. "Yup, Lilly just stood there. What'd you do to her? Seems to me a woman would have lifted a hand to catch a boo-kay if she wanted to get married."

"Yep, I think you're probably right about that, sir."

"Well, son, I'll tell you it was a good thing she didn't catch the flowers. That gal that did went down under a herd of brawlers. I think everybody came up with a petal."

"I don't know about coming up with a petal, but I know they were wearin' them in their hair," added Stanley.

"All I can say in their defense is that the cowboys didn't act much better when Clint threw that pink hatband. Yep, Lacy designed that thang all special like with them words proclamating "I'm next" stitched across it. Yep, quite unusual, but there's a few black eyes this morning over that little piece of elastic. And onliest one fella wearing it around his hat." Applegate popped a few seeds into his mouth. Cort figured he'd grown tired of waiting till he got over to Sam's to chomp on the little fellas.

"In their defense," rambled Stanley—he was on a roll, too—"there were a few ladies that remained out of the scramble. Those nice teachers living over at Adela's didn't get into it—matter of·fact, none of the ladies already living here got into the fight. They was real ladies about the whole thang and let them that wanted to brawl have at it. Can't say I blame 'em. It ain't like that boo-kay-catchin' thang is ever accurate."

Cort had about lost patience, and stepped up to the counter. Pete grabbed his pen from behind his ear and took his order while Stanley and Applegate eased up behind him.

"What you need all that alfalfa for?"

Cort looked to his right at Applegate. "For my stock."

"Leroy always ordered a ton of that stuff, too. Said his jack—"

"Donkey." Cort cut in on Stanley. "Samantha prefers burro or donkey to the biblically correct name."

Stanley scratched his head. "That's exactly what Leroy used to say about that donkey. She been letting your stock loose?"

"Yep."

"She's a stinker. Leroy used to get mad enough to spit nails at that little donkey," Applegate said, setting his bag of seeds down.

That wasn't a good sign for Cort. He figured this was going to be another long story, and he really needed to go.

"Said to us many times that he raised that donkey to sell as a nursemaid to livestock, and he'd have sold her many times over just to get her out of his hair. But he couldn't do it, seeins how that sweet, lonesome Lilly needed something to love. And she shore nuff did love that Samantha. Ain't that right, Stanley?"

Cort's heart started thumping hard in his chest just thinking about Lilly needing something to love. He felt bad standing in the feed store listening to gossip about her and was glad when Pete came out with his order and they could go outside and load it into the back of his truck.

The two older men followed them.

Cort didn't hang around and encourage any more talk about Lilly. It was exactly as he'd thought. Lilly needed a large family to make up for all the years of loneliness she'd endured growing up. No matter how cute Samantha was, Lilly needed more than a donkey to love. She needed children and a husband who would love her the way she deserved.

Lilly stepped from the barn and ran a hand through her hair. It was a beautiful day. A robin ate feed off the ground near the door, promising that spring was soon approaching. Lilly stretched her arms above her head and arched her back to ease the strain of having unloaded the forty-pound sacks of feed from her pickup to the feed room. It felt good to be getting back in shape, but she'd very nearly overdone it today.

Walking to the gate, she propped one booted foot on the bottom rung and leaned her arms on the top rung as she watched her cattle grazing in the distance. The baby monitor was sitting on the hood of her truck to alert her when Joshua awakened from his afternoon nap. It was a good day. It would be a perfect day if…

Tears pricked her eyes, then she lowered her head in prayer. It was the only way she could find peace from the heartache plaguing her. From the what-ifs. There was no solution unless God stepped in and changed either her heart or Cort's. She'd realized the night of the reception when she'd watched Cort leave minutes after she and Bob had come in from the cold that she might not get her wish.

Her heart hadn't been into the rest of the evening. It was as if it had walked out with Cort. Even when the fight broke out over the bouquet she hadn't felt much. Let them fight over who would be the next wife of Mule Hollow. Unless God changed Cort's heart, she would never marry again.

But she knew she had a calling and she was blessed to have it. Raising a child to love the Lord was the most important thing she could do. Her highest calling. The world needed more godly men. She had begun diligently seeking God's wisdom and guidance in building her personal relationship with Him. She wanted her heart to be fully prepared to guide Joshua as he grew. If God chose to bless her with a godly husband, then He would. She had peace, along with a few tears at times, but still she had peace knowing she was on the path God wanted her to be on.

If it was to be, then it would be. God was in control. Her insides were still turned upside down, though.

Thank You, Lord, for blessing me so. For giving me a son, good friends who shared Your love with me and have pulled me into their fold. I am truly blessed. I thank You for giving me such a wonderful place to raise Joshua and such wonderful godly people to look up to as I endeavor to do Your will in this calling. Thank You, Father. I pray all these things asking that Your will be done. Amen.

Lilly laid her head on her crossed arms and relaxed, watching the cattle mill around in the distance. They worried about nothing. Their food was provided, their welfare taken care of, by her, their caretaker. Lilly knew Joshua's and her welfare was being taken care of by the best caretaker there was.

Looking at her watch, she started walking toward the front of her driveway. Bob was supposed to be showing up any minute to start the new single-pole gate he was welding for her. It was an easy fix for her Samantha problem. With the gate in place Samantha could continue to have the run of the place without being able to get out on the dirt road. Thus she'd be unable to go down to Cort's and cause any more problems.

She, on the other hand, needed to see Cort. She was dedicating Joshua to the Lord on Sunday, and also wanted to announce that Cort was Joshua's godparent. She needed to make certain he still wanted the responsibility and that he would be at the service with her.

She hadn't considered how uncomfortable standing up there with him would be.

She hadn't really thought about a lot of things when she'd asked Cort to be Joshua's guardian. In the event that something did happen to her, it was crucial that Joshua be comfortable in the new environment with his guardian. With Cort. That meant Lilly might have to be around Cort more than she could—no, she could handle anything. Cort was her friend. Nothing more. And she could handle this. With God's help she could.

That is, if Cort still wanted Joshua.

Cort was in the barn when he heard Loser go bonkers. Samantha was on the premises. Coming out of the barn, Cort saw her back end as she disappeared inside his house.

"Samantha!" Cort yelled, not certain why he even attempted to call out to her. It was as if she was deaf by choice. Loser was barking inside and Cort could hear crashing in the few seconds it took him to get to the back door. One look inside and he was ready to…well, he wasn't ready to shoot her or anything, but he was ready to sell her. Even if she didn't belong to him.

His temper was short anyway and the disastrous donkey tearing up his kitchen was the last thing he needed.

Yanking open the door, he stormed into the kitchen just in time to witness Samantha knocking the toaster to the floor as she wrapped her chubby lips around the bread bag and squeezed. The bag popped and bread blew out the end. Several pieces hit Loser on the head, causing him to jump, and run into Samantha's legs as the donkey spun toward the door—knocking his coffeemaker off the counter as she swung her bread-bag-filled mouth around.

The moment Samantha saw him, he figured she knew she was in big trouble.

Lilly was expecting Bob when she saw Cort's truck making slow progress toward her. Tied to the tailgate was Samantha. One look at Cort's scowling face told her Samantha had been up to no good. Again.

"Get in," he snapped, coming to a halt beside her. Lilly didn't ask questions. She could tell by the contrite look on Samantha's long face that he probably had good reason to be upset.

"I'm afraid to ask what happened," she said, slamming the door. Loser bounded into her lap with a joyous yelp and immediately tried to lick her to death.

"Loser, down, boy!" she exclaimed as Cort gave the truck gas. "Don't you pet this dog?" she squealed, trying to get a handle on the excited pooch.

Cort only grunted and kept on driving. Well, she wasn't thrilled to see him, either. Except she did have to ask him the guardian question.

He brought the truck to a halt beside the barn and wasted no time getting out. Lilly followed, allowing Loser to hop to the ground after her. When she rounded the end of the truck Cort was untying Samantha from the tailgate.

Lilly heard Joshua cry from the baby monitor. Time to get his bottle. "I'll be right back and you can tell me what happened."

Another grunt. Jogging to the house, Lilly grabbed a bottle from the fridge, placed it in the microwave, then dashed down the hall to get her baby.

When she exited the house a few minutes later with Joshua in her arms, happily smacking away on his bottle, she could hear Cort clanging around in the barn.

"What is that man doing?"

He was in fact busy fixing the wooden gate that used to work but had broken years ago. She hadn't needed the barn to be closed off and yes, if the gate worked, then Samantha would be limited to exiting into the pasture versus the yard.

But Samantha *liked* being in the yard.

"I should have fixed this weeks ago," he mumbled.

He was muttering again. Lilly hid a smile. He was so adorably cute when frustrated. An instant replay flashed through her memory of the first night in his barn when he'd been so mad at having lassoed a pregnant woman. That night standing in her cold barn, she'd wished for a man, any man. But God had sent her Cort. Not just any man, but the right man for her.

His blue eyes were screaming exasperation, flashing brilliantly in the clear February sunlight. She loved this man.

Yep, no mistaking it. She loved him.

"Do you have a hammer?"

She wanted to throw her arms around his neck and tell him how much he meant to her. She wanted to scare him to death if that was what it took to make him realize he was what she wanted.

"In fact, I do," she said instead as a giggle bubbled out of her. "And hello to you, too."

He looked up from the rusted hinge he was trying to

pry loose from the gate and had the decency to look embarrassed by his rude behavior.

"Hello," he said politely, his gaze darting to Joshua. "He's growing."

"Babies do have a tendency to do that. Quickly."

He frowned, his eyes lingering on her baby before rising to her. Lilly's pulse picked up.

"Yeah, they grow up fast. So I'm told."

Lilly's heart swelled with sympathy for him. He so wanted children. She knew he loved Joshua, but...*please, Father, let him love me, too.* "Follow me, and I'll show you where the hammer is. Sorry I haven't fixed the fence. What did she do this time?" She could barely keep her voice steady.

"Instead of breaking and entering, she entered and broke my kitchen."

"Oh, no!" Lilly stopped and turned toward him. "I'm really sorry. I'll come help clean everything up and then I'll replace anything she broke."

"It's no big deal."

Lilly started toward the tack room, sidestepping when Loser scrambled past her. *What in the world!* Looking over her shoulder, she saw the dog skid to a stop beside Samantha, who was leaning against the door watching everything with big wide eyes. Her long ears twitched and her fuzzy tail swished in a rhythmic motion that reminded Lilly of a cat about to pounce on an unsuspecting mouse.

The little stinker was not in the least repentant about her activities. Well, that was about to change, because Cort was fixing the gate and Bob was going to weld her another gate at the entrance to her drive. That should curb Samantha's wanderings.

The small tack room was dark as Lilly stepped into it. "The light switch is that string there," she said, lifting her chin upward, indicating where Cort should reach up and pull.

He followed her into the cramped space and grabbed the string just as Lilly heard a familiar sound.

The creaking of the tack-room door as it slammed, shutting them inside.

"What!" Cort spun around as the mellow light illuminated the four walls and the sturdy wooden door.

Lilly didn't think much of it at first. The wind had blown it shut. But there was no wind.

Cort immediately twisted the handle and pushed, but it didn't budge. He put his broad shoulder to the door and put all his strength into it. Still the door held fast.

"Has this happened before?"

"No."

From beyond the door they could hear Loser barking, and then from just outside the door they heard the very familiar *Eee-haw* of Samantha.

"Samantha!"

Chapter Twenty-Four

They coaxed, they begged, but nothing would budge the portly scalawag from her post in front of the door.

After Cort had pushed until there was no pushing left in him, Lilly handed Joshua over and peeked out the crack between the door and the wall. If she maneuvered herself just so, she could look over and see Samantha quietly lounging against the door munching on a piece of straw. Loser had settled down beside her with his chin resting on his crossed front paws.

"I'm telling you, it's as if they're at a sit-in, like protests people organize. You know, where the people sit down and won't budge until their requirements are met, and they get what they want." Lilly turned toward Cort, very aware of his nearness. Her heart clunked against her stomach at the picture he made as he ignored her every word. He was totally, beautifully lost in making faces at a contented Joshua.

So much for being desperate to escape, as he'd first acted.

Why, she'd have sworn he was terrified at the thought of being trapped in a small space with her.

After the first shock of their situation she was actually happy at the prospect.

Really, what could be better than being trapped with the two people she loved most in the world? Nothing. It was an answer to prayer—

Oh, my goodness!

She swallowed the yelp of happiness that almost escaped her and thanked the good Lord for this odd turn of events.

Cort's hat was pushed back from his forehead and his black hair peeked out from beneath it in a messy fringe. He really needed a haircut, but what else was new? He'd needed a haircut for a month and she'd grown used to the longer length. She'd grown used to everything about him. The way he smiled at her when he first saw her and the way he stuck his fingertips into the front pockets of his jeans. The way he strode across a room or an expanse as if he were on a mission. The way he laughed…oh, the way he laughed. It never ceased to bless her heart to hear the sound of his deep gravelly chuckle.

"I guess we just sit and wait," she said, ramming a hand through her hair. "Samantha has to move sometime. And if she doesn't, Bob is supposed to be here any moment."

Cort placed Joshua against his chest, letting the baby's head rest on his shoulder. He'd become so comfortable with Joshua.

"Bob? Are you dating him?" Cort glanced up from Joshua inquisitively.

"No. Bob's my friend. He's coming to build a fence down at the road."

"The two of you seemed to be close at the reception. I thought maybe—"

"We're friends, Cort," Lilly said firmly, then pushed away from the door and walked toward him. Her pulse pounded in her ears. Maybe the small space was the reason she thought she'd heard a hint of jealousy in his voice. She stopped just a step away from him.

"I was going to come and ask you again…I mean, we never did completely get the matter of your being Joshua's guardian settled."

"I told you I would. But nothing's going to happen to you."

"We don't know that. God doesn't promise us tomorrow. And as a good mother I have to look out for Joshua even in the event that I should be taken home to be with God."

"Why do you want me? Just because I helped deliver Joshua doesn't mean I'd be the best one to raise him."

"Yes, you helped deliver him and that gives you a bond with him. And with me. But I know you would raise him to love the Lord and to put God first. To always strive to walk with God. Those are the most important reasons." Lilly's voice broke. She willed away the tears stinging the back of her eyes. She wanted to be strong. She didn't want Cort's pity.

"How do you know that I would do that?" The question was just a hoarse whisper. His blue eyes were bright with bridled emotions. Emotions, Lilly knew, he'd tried to bury. Hopes he'd tried to tame.

She couldn't help herself—she touched his arm. The one wrapped around her sweet baby. So secure. So reassuring.

"Cort, you had something terrible happen to you.

You had your dreams stripped away because of something completely out of your control." She sniffed. "But you didn't turn away from God. You held on to Him. Even in your pain."

"But I was angry."

"Anger is a normal reaction. God expects and understands anger. I read yesterday the passage where it says be angry and sin not. I respect so much that you came to a quiet place to be still and to know what God had in store for you. Even in your anger you did what you needed to do to be in God's will."

Please give me the right words, Lord.

A tear slipped down her cheek. "He led you to me."

"Lilly, I can't—"

She placed three fingers on his lips. She had to say this. "The other reasons I want you to be Joshua's guardian are because you love him already and because you need him as much as he is going to need you. I'm— I'm not asking you to love me. I understand, in a weird way, that…" Her heart was breaking. Maybe she was reading God's will wrong. Maybe Cort was here only to be by Joshua's side. Maybe she was meant to be alone. Maybe the Tipps women had a destiny that was always going to stay the same. She hugged herself and stepped away from Cort.

Cort's heart was tearing apart. The look of hope and love in Lilly's expression wrapped around him, tearing at his resolve.

"Lilly, I can't give you more children." Didn't she understand that? "In the terms of the grannies, I'm worthless."

Lilly's eyes flashed. "My grannies, except for

Granny Bunches, let bitterness color their world. Over time bitterness can warp people's thoughts, so much so that they can't see straight. So that they choose their own fate. I see that very clearly now. I don't want my life ruled by what the grannies told me. I want God's truths to color my world. In His terms you are priceless. And you are priceless…to me."

Cort took a step toward Lilly. He loved her. He'd been kidding himself. He couldn't let Lilly go without a fight. She was more precious to him than jewels. And Joshua…looking into Joshua's innocent face, Cort knew he wanted to be this child's daddy. He wanted to be the one to teach Joshua to tie his shoes. He wanted to hold Joshua's hand when they walked down to the pond to catch his first fish. He wanted to teach Joshua to ride a horse and he wanted Joshua to call him Dad. He wanted to be more than his guardian…. Lilly said he was priceless to God and to her. Could God have given him such a gift?

Looking into Lilly's beautiful face, knowing how special her spirit was, he felt hope flare inside him. He wanted to be the one who came home to Lilly at night. He wanted to love her for all of his days.

His pulse was tap-dancing against his temple. "I can't give you more children." He had to warn her again. She deserved so much more.

"I only want the children God intends me to have." Lilly took a step toward him. Her eyes were bright and steady. "I love you, Cort. Could you love me?"

The break in her voice and the sudden questions in her eyes broke all his defenses. Did she think she was unlovable?

No hesitations now—Cort saw why God had brought him here. "I love you, Lilly. I've loved you from the beginning." He wrapped his free arm around her and pulled her close. She came willingly, and his world was right. As he held her and Joshua, his heart surged with emotion. "Lilly, I can't give you more children, but I promise you that I'll love you and Joshua with all my heart for as long as God will let me. And if you want to adopt more children, then we will."

Tears glistened in Lilly's eyes as Cort bent and touched his lips to hers. She wrapped her arms around his neck and he knew he was home. He was with the woman God had intended for him all along. He was blessed.

Thank You, God.

God had given him back his dream.

Lilly surrounded by children surfaced in his mind.

Trust me.

And he did. They were kissing when the tack-room door squeaked open. Cort and Lilly rested their foreheads together and turned to see Samantha with her big lips wrapped around the door handle like a kid with a lollipop stuck in its mouth. Loser sat on his haunches, his tail wiggling back and forth, his eyes expectant.

Cort kissed Lilly's ear. "I think that donkey had this planned all along."

Lilly touched Cort's face, for the first time allowing the sensation to fill her fully. "I think you might be right."

"Lilly, will you marry me?"

She kissed Joshua's cheek, then kissed Cort soundly on the lips. "I thought you'd never ask. Yes. Yes. And yes."

Samantha pawed the earth, drawing their attention as she lifted her chin, rolled back her lips, exposed her big pearly whites and let an earsplitting *Eee-haw* explode.

Loser yelped his agreement, nipped at Samantha's

knee, then took off running with Samantha trotting after him.

Cort and Lilly burst into laughter.

"You do know we have to give Loser a new name?" Lilly said, gazing up into Cort's eyes.

Cort let her love wash over him, renewing him. "Oh, yeah. There are no losers around here anymore."

And then he kissed her.

Epilogue

Lilly scanned the crowd outside the church, her gaze finding Cort holding Joshua close, like a pro. They were surrounded by a throng of well-wishers led by Norma Sue, Esther Mae and Adela. Lilly's heart swelled with pride at seeing *her guys* together.

The wedding had been over for an hour and she still couldn't believe she was Mrs. Cort Wells. Who'd a-thunk it? Lilly Tipps married—to the right man this time! "Well grannies, it looks like our luck has finally changed," she whispered to herself, knowing without doubt that Cort's love was forever hers.

"Talking to yourself already?"

Lilly turned to find her maid of honor grinning at her. "Hey, Lacy, you caught me chatting to the grannies about my new husband. Surely they're smiling right now."

"I'm sure they are. I know I am. I'm so happy for you. It's so cool how God brought the two of you together."

"Not too many women can boast that her hero rode to her rescue on the back of a little donkey with a grumpy dog in tow." Lilly laughed, thinking back to the night Joshua was born.

Lacy laughed, too. "I don't think Joshua is going to believe us when we tell him the tale of his birth."

"Just think, Lacy. It's like I waited all these years and then Cort showed up just at the right time."

"God's time," Lacy added. "His timing is always perfect."

Lilly's heart skipped as Cort came striding up to stand beside her. Lacy immediately snatched Joshua away and started making faces at him as he gazed at her frilly blond hair with wide eyes.

"What's perfect?" Cort asked, giving Lilly a lingering kiss.

"This," she said, spreading her arms wide to encompass the gathering of friends. "I feel like I'm in a fairy tale." Her eyes brimmed with tears of happiness. "I love you so much, Cort. I never dreamed this could really happen to me." He put his arms around her and drew her against him in a solid embrace that she never wanted to end.

"I was thinking the same thing," he said. "I never dreamed my life could be so blessed. You make me the happiest man alive, Lilly. Are you ready to load up and head out?"

"I am so ready. Are you sure Samantha and Lucky will be okay while we're gone?"

"Yes, they'll be fine. Bob will check on them every day. Now that Samantha is back on her old stomping grounds, she's as happy as a clam. And Loser—I mean Lucky—is like a new dog. He's so happy to have a friend that he won't even notice we're gone. I still can't believe you wanted to combine our honeymoon with a horse show."

Lilly touched his cheek. "Why not? I'm looking forward to seeing your world, and Oklahoma seems like a good place to start. Besides, I'm getting to meet all of your family. Just think, Cort, we're a family."

"Family," he said, tracing the outline of her face with his fingertips. "I do like the sound of that, Mrs. Wells."

"Yep, kind of a weird family," Lacy chimed in, holding Joshua high in the air as she looked up at his cherubic face. "Samantha, Lucky, Lilly, Cort and baby makes five. That's right, you cute little fella, I have the feeling that you're going to have one unusual upbringing."

Lilly laughed at that bit of insight and leaned her head against Cort's shoulder, loving the way she felt wrapped in her husband's strong arms. "One thing's for certain," she said, tilting her head and meeting his laughing eyes. "Our life won't be boring."

Cort smiled that smile of his that touched Lilly all the way to the tips of her tingling toes. "As long as it's with you, Lilly, it sounds perfect to me."

* * * * *

Dear Reader,

I hope you enjoyed reading Lilly's and Cort's story. The idea for this book started building in my mind the day I went to a friend's home to dye her horse black... yes, I dyed a horse black from the tip of his ears to the tops of his hooves! While there I encountered the *real* Samantha. She was a bumpy little burro full of mischief and fun, and the moment I watched her in action, I knew I was going to create a story around a character similar to her. My sons were small back then and loved dogs and donkeys, among other animals, so I created Samantha and Loser specifically to make them laugh. Each night at bedtime I would read the scenes involving the pesky critters, and their laughter still warms my heart when I think about it.

I hope God blesses you in a special way today and that I was able to be a part of that with the telling of this story in some small way. Until next time I pray that through all of life you hold fast to the Lord. You can contact me at P.O. Box 1125, Madisonville, Texas 77864, and please visit my Web site, www.debraclopton.com.

In Christ's Love,

Debra Clopton

QUESTIONS FOR DISCUSSION

1. The Bible says be angry and sin not. Cort had many things to be angry about, but he still kept his faith. What are your thoughts on his reactions?

2. Do you sometimes feel like Job and that God is allowing Satan to test your faith? Do you ever feel your life is falling apart and God expects you to smile and accept it without complaint? What advice have you received that helped you? Were there Scripture verses you found particularly appropriate?

3. Lilly realized that she had a major responsibility when it came to raising her child. How do you think the world would change if more parents took their responsibility seriously?

4. The theme verse for *And Baby Makes Five* is, "Teach me to do Your will, for You are my God; may Your good spirit lead me on level ground." Psalms 143:10. Does God *teach* us to do His good will? How?

5. As a new Christian, Lilly had much in her upbringing to sift through in order to find level ground. Why is it important for a new Christian to have guidance from mature Christians in order to grasp a full understanding of the Bible? How do we all benefit from guidance?

6. Through no fault of his own, Cort's bright future as he knew it was shattered. Do you know someone struggling to find God's will in the midst of tragedy? Are you?

7. Lilly's views are shaped by the thoughts of those who raised her. How hard is it to break the cycle of your upbringing? How easy is it to judge someone whose life views you don't understand?

8. Have you seen God fulfill His will through odd circumstances or use unusual people or animals to achieve His goal? Please share.

BE MY NEAT-HEART

BY

JUDY BAER

*A Special
Steeple Hill Café Novel
in Love Inspired*

Everything in
professional organizer
Sammi Smith's life was
perfect—except her love
life. That all changed
after she met fellow
neatnik Jared Hamilton,
who'd hired her to help
with his sister's "clutter
issues." Sometimes love
can be a messy business!

*Available May 2006
wherever you buy books.*

Steeple
Hill
Café

www.SteepleHill.com

LIBMN